This book is dedicated to:
Elise, Sasha, Kirah, Alicia, Tiekela, Alexis,
Arondra, Lauren, Ebony, Sonia, Maiya,
Kenya, Shaila, Kyra and Alex B.
Do great things!

ms. Thang

by Sonia Hayes

N.U.A

NATIONAL
UNDERGROUND
ASSOCIATION

Published by
NUA Multimedia, LLC
PMB #309
4611 Hardscrabble Road #109
Columbia, SC 29229

Cover design by: Diane Florence
Author Portrait: Ron MacDonald

ISBN: 0-9777573-0-7

LCCN: 2006921393

Acknowledgments

A special thank you to my super trooper, AEP4, you have been a wonderful support and motivator. (Who loves ya'!) To my number one fan and reader, Elise, much love. A million thanks to my grandmother for everything, (I really was listening when I was a teenager and you were RIGHT, "there is nothing new under the sun".) Thanks to AEP3 for the quick edit. Many thanks to my writing group buddies at Pickneyville Writers Group, Sandhills Writers Group and Columbia II, your input was invaluable. Thanks to my editor, Ann K. Fisher. Last but not least, a special thank you to all the readers for your support.

ms. Thang

Chapter 1

"Brittany! Natasha!" Shaniqua yelled down the noisy hallway.

"I swear, Tasha, that girl is just like school in the summertime, no class," Brittany whispered as Shaniqua approached them.

"Hey hey hey, what's happenin' y'all?" Shaniqua said, swinging her shoulder-length micro braids out of her face, while smacking on chewing gum.

"Hi, Shaniqua, how was your summer?" Natasha asked, leaning in for a hug.

"Dang Tasha, you grew a lot," Shaniqua said, looking up at Natasha. "My summer vacation was off the chain, girl. I hung out with my cousin, Renee. You know, the one we call Nee Nee, who just turned twenty-one. We had a ball hanging out with some fine boys this summer. Whew!" Shaniqua said, fanning herself. "How was yours?"

"Mine was good," Natasha replied, crouching forward, trying to lessen the height gap. "I mostly played basketball with my brothers. I'm trying out for the JV team this year."

Shaniqua looked to Brittany. "How 'bout you, Ms. Thang? What you can't show nobody love?"

Brittany leaned her upper body in slightly, but kept her butt poking out as she gave Shaniqua a weak hug. "I went to Europe with my parents for a month, came back and practiced piano, and just hung out."

Shaniqua inspected Brittany from head to toe, then smirked. "You obviously were eating good too, huh?"

Brittany rolled her eyes and pursed her lips. "Whatever."

The bell sounded to begin the first day of school at Miller Grove High.

"Dang, too bad we don't have classes together," Shaniqua said.

Natasha smiled. "Well, at least we all have fourth period lunch together."

"True that, true that. Girls, we're sexy sophomores and it's time to get the party crunk! I've got a plan to become the 'It' girls this year. I've got to go, but we'll talk at lunch," Shaniqua said, sashaying her shapely, petite frame toward homeroom.

Brittany watched Shaniqua disappear into the thick crowd. "What in the world does she think she's doing with those colored eye contacts? She looks like some kind of wild feline and chewing gum like she's chomping on rocks," Brittany said, shaking her head to make her long black wavy locks sway across her back. "That's your friend, not mine. Thank God we don't have any classes together."

"You're in honors again this year?" Natasha asked.

"Of course, my dad wouldn't have it any other way," Brittany said.

"Okay girl, see you at lunch."

"Write me a note."

Natasha Harris sat in homeroom with her knees cramped underneath the desk. She had grown several inches over the summer. It was inevitable she would inherit her father's height. Being home, surrounded by her dad and two brothers, always made her feel normal. It wasn't until she got to school that she felt like the big, green man on the vegetable can. Natasha knew she was tall, already 5'10", and being a tall girl in high school was not cool. She hated towering over everyone in class, including some teachers. But not being able to fit comfortably in her desk was more than she could bear this year. If only they didn't make these dang chairs connected to the desk, she thought.

"Good morning class, my name is Ms. Andrews. I see a few familiar faces," she said, grinning at Natasha. "I trust you all had a great vacation and kept up with your summer reading list."

A few moans resonated from the back of the room.

"Natasha, can I get you to help me, please?" Ms. Andrews said, motioning for her to come to the front of the classroom.

Natasha sat there stunned. Her eyes locked unintentionally with Stephen Perry, then quickly stole back to Ms. Andrews. She had no desire to become her pet just because her brother Nathan had been in her class last year. Everyone knew Ms. Andrews was a big pain. What's more, she had a big doublewide for a butt that could hardly fit into her seat and a squeaky voice that made your ears ring. The students always joked that's why she didn't have a husband.

"Yes ma'am," Natasha said, getting up to walk to the front of the class. *Ho, ho, ho, green giant!* She felt as though all eyes were on her and she really was becoming the vegetable man with each step taken, her medium brown complexion slowly turning olive green.

She pretended not to hear the snickering. She focused her thoughts on more pleasant things, like hearing Shaniqua's plan at lunchtime to become the "It" girls. Then they would be snickering out of envy, and they'd be the ones turning green.

Fourth period lunch, the cafeteria was bursting with noise from every direction. The August heat in Atlanta made eating outside impossible. The girls settled for a table toward the back entrance of the lunchroom.

"No, see, that's the problem," Shaniqua said, shaking her head. "Why y'all sittin' all the way back here where the whack kids sit? We did that last year, and my cousin, Nee Nee, said if we want to change our reputation, then it would have to be done now, in the tenth grade. I ain't sitting back here no more."

"Shaniqua, there aren't any seats up front," Brittany said, stuffing fries in her mouth.

"Let's get folks to move over," Shaniqua said.

Brittany's brows puckered. "It's not that serious for me."

"We need to talk in private anyway, so let's just stay here for now," Natasha said.

"Y'all will never guess who's in my homeroom?" Shaniqua said picking over her food, "Fine ass Jordan Kelley."

"How's he in your homeroom, when he's supposed to be a junior this year?" Brittany asked.

"I don't know, and I don't care, fine as he is."

Brittany offered a critical smirk. "He can be as fine as he wants to be, but he's dumb."

"Now see, there you go Brittany, always puttin' people down. Sorry, not everybody can be in honors like you, Ms. Perfect," Shaniqua scoffed. "Really, you don't know why he's in my homeroom."

"Because he flunked last year. It's not rocket science, Shaniqua. Well, maybe it is for you."

"You really get on my last freakin' --!"

"All right, just chill," Natasha interrupted. "So what's this plan you have for us to become "It" girls this year?"

"Nee Nee said, 'In order to be popular in school you have to have the right friends.'" Shaniqua looked at Brittany. "I ain't gonna hold that against you."

"Puh-leeze, you should be so lucky."

"And she said 'You have to dress the part, but most of all, you have to date the right guys.' How y'all like my new look?" Shaniqua asked, showing off her aqua blue mini skirt, black V-neck knit top and matching stilettos. "Nee Nee hooked me up... tight right?" Shaniqua struck a dramatic pose with one hand on a cocked hip and the other, pressed gently on the side of her face.

Brittany eyed Natasha then turned her head in the opposite direction, trying to conceal laughter.

"Well, you look like you're ready for some action," Natasha said, trying not to embarrass her friend whom she had known since elementary school.

"Perfect, thank you, that's the response I was looking for," Shaniqua said, flaunting her new look.

Brittany sniggered, pretending to be engrossed in her food. Brittany and Natasha became friends last year in French class, and by association, Brittany and Shaniqua tolerated one another. Brittany could no longer hold it in. "Natasha please, you know you need to quit it. You know Shaniqua looks like she just got finished booty shaking in the latest rap video."

"Don't hate, appreciate," Shaniqua chimed.

"Girl, please, my dad would kill me if I walked out the house dressed like that," Brittany said. "You need to go shopping with us."

"I will, 'cause y'all need help," Shaniqua said,

then turned her back to Brittany, and continued talking to Natasha. "Now, for the boys, I got my eye on Jordan Kelley. I saw him checking me out in homeroom. He will be mine, watch."

"Humph!" Brittany flashed a critical smirk. "Dressed like that, everybody's going to be checking you out, Ms. Thang."

"Seriously, Shaniqua, you need to be careful, I heard some pretty nasty things about him," Natasha said.

Shaniqua looked defiantly at Natasha. "Nothing I can't handle. Humph, I refuse to have lame high school years."

Chapter 2

Saturday afternoon, the air was stifling as Brittany Brown sat in the backseat of the car. It was so hot, she felt like she was breathing in air from a hot oven. Perspiration beaded on Brittany's forehead as they sat parked in front of Shaniqua's duplex house. She hoped she wouldn't sweat out her fresh hairdo. She wanted to plead with Natasha's brother, Nate, to turn on the air-conditioner, but Natasha had already said that he wouldn't because it burned too much gas. Just when Brittany decided to wait outside the car, Shaniqua appeared at the front door wearing a black mini, a red and white striped spandex top and black stilettos.

"Oh, no, I'm not about to walk in Lenox Mall with her dressed like a hoochie. Y'all can take me home," Brittany said.

Natasha turned to face Brittany in the back seat, then whispered, "You're forgetting the purpose of our shopping trip, remember? We're trying to show

Shaniqua that she can look cute without dressing...
Oh hey, Shaniqua, girl."

"Hey hey hey, what's happenin' y'all?"

"What's up?" Nate said.

Brittany flashed a fake smile and slid her sleek
mane gracefully behind her ear. "Shaniqua, you
know Lenox is the mall where celebrities shop and
everybody goes to be seen."

"I know, I hope we see somebody famous,"
Shaniqua said enthusiastically.

Brittany tucked her arms tightly across her
chest and shook her head, repressing the desire to
shout, then why in the hell are you dressed like
that? But she didn't want to upset Natasha.
Secretly, she wondered why Natasha continued to
befriend Shaniqua. She had always thought that
maybe Natasha felt guilty because Shaniqua was
being raised by her grandmother and never
mentioned her parents. Brittany gazed out the
window, her mother's words echoing in her head,
'Birds of a feather flock together.' Now, everyone in
the mall would be looking at her sideways, too.

The traffic was thick on Peachtree Street.
Luxury cars and hoopties alike spilled onto the
four-lane street, while pedestrians crammed the
sidewalks. All of Atlanta was on the move.
Peachtree Street was the strip, which ran from
downtown through Buckhead and out until it
turned into Peachtree Industrial Boulevard;

everything in Atlanta related to a peachtree in one way or another. Buckhead was where everyone wanted to work, shop, eat or catch a movie. Hotels were stacked high on every corner, a host of eateries with patrons dining on the patio-lined streets. Phipps Plaza, a choice shopping destination for the truly affluent, was adjacent to Lenox, thereby creating traffic jams seven days a week. At night, the hip crowd cruised the strip with their music bumping, while slushed partygoers went club hopping on foot.

After nearly thirty minutes of traveling bumper to bumper, Nate turned off Peachtree Street and into the shopping mall. The parking lot was full, even valet parking had no more spaces left for the mostly exotic vehicles. People of all races and social status meandered to and from the building.

"Be ready at four o'clock." Nate told the girls.

Natasha frowned. "That only leaves three hours to shop," she protested as she stepped out of their father's silver Buick Century.

"All right by me," Shaniqua said. "I don't have no money no way. I'm just excited to be here." Shaniqua rushed toward the entrance.

Using her acquired ballet skills, Brittany stepped out of the car gracefully, showing off her French pedicure in brown snakeskin sandals, and thanked her chauffeur.

"Four o'clock," Nate reiterated and pulled away.

Brittany led the girls inside. She had been to this mall more times than she could count.

Brittany took for granted what most girls only dreamed about: weekly shopping sprees. It was her mom's raison d'etre to keep up with the latest fashions. Her mom settled for Lenox and Phipps when she couldn't get to Paris or New York. It was their Saturday ritual to be at the hairdresser's at nine o'clock and then spend the afternoon lunching and shopping. Brittany couldn't remember missing a weekly hair appointment since she turned five.

Brittany was an attractive girl, full-figured, with bold curves. She had fine features that could have easily been borrowed from her white counterpart. Her brown eyes were full and round, almost doll-like, which made her look sweet. Brittany had all the outward manifestations of a true "Southern belle." She was very polite when she needed to be. She knew how to make her dimples dance when she wanted to charm. But most times she acted like she was better than everyone because her dad was a prominent heart surgeon.

"So this is Lenox?" Shaniqua said, inspecting one of the hottest shopping destinations in the Southeast. She felt at home with the attractive women and teenagers parading around in high-heels, and their hair styled to perfection. Finally, she knew why everyone wanted to hang out there. The mall was like a fashion show with men and women competing alike.

"Where do you guys want to go first?" Brittany asked.

"I just want to walk the mall and check out the boys," Shaniqua said. "Tasha, isn't that Stephen Perry over there?"

"Where?" Tasha and Brittany said in unison, looking around.

Shaniqua pointed. "Right there in the shoe store. Y'all blind?"

"No, we're not, hawk eyes," Brittany said.

"Uh-huh, didn't somebody have the hots for Stephen last year?" Shaniqua teased.

"I did not," Natasha said.

"Did to. You don't have to lie, Ms. Thang," Shaniqua said. "Truth or Dare?"

Natasha puckered her lips into a nasty smirk. "We are not twelve years old."

"Okay, Tasha, if you don't like him, then go over and speak to him," Brittany said.

Natasha shook her head. "For what? I see him every day at school. He's in my homeroom and art class this year."

Brittany giggled, "Uh-huh, you didn't tell us."

Natasha shrugged. "Whatever." She hated when Brittany started her giggling fits. Nothing in life was that frickin' amusing.

"Well, do it just to be nice," Brittany said, batting her eyelids, and smiling, revealing beautifully straightened teeth that could only come from years of enduring metal. "You know, that ol' southern hospitality," Brittany mimicked in perfect southern diction.

"It's no big deal," Natasha said.

"Don't sing it, bring it, Ms. Thang," Shaniqua sang.

Natasha rolled her eyes, then drew in a lungful of air. She started her journey across the mall, silently praying for a wave of courage. Her height was steadily increasing by the inch with each step taken. *Ho ho ho, green giant.* Her nerves were at an all time high. She only hoped they wouldn't silence her indefinitely. She turned back to look at her friends. *Evil witches.* Her palms were clammy. *God, I hope he doesn't want to high-five. No silly, he'd want to shake your hand. Oh, I'm going to get them. Oh, God, he's looking this way.* Natasha smiled like it hurt. "Hey, Stephen."

"What's up?"

"Nothing."

A long, uncomfortable silence lingered.

"Just getting some school supplies, I mean art supplies. Well not here, but ..." Natasha said.

"Who are you here with?" Stephen asked.

Natasha turned around and pointed. "My girlfriends."

Shaniqua and Brittany waved, then let out a loud burst of giggles. The kind of giggles that alerted teenage boys that someone had a crush on them. *I'm going to clank their heads together.*

"Well, my dad's waiting. I'll catch you on Monday," Stephen smiled.

"Bye," Natasha mumbled, from sheer lack of anything more profound to say. She made her way back across the mall, embarrassment burning her face. Her long slender fingers wiped gobs of sweat from her forehead.

Brittany giggled. "You weren't nervous were you, Mrs. Perry?"

Brittany and Shaniqua doubled over with laughter, holding their stomachs.

Natasha nearly rolled her eyes and neck off her shoulders. "I swear, y'all are so embarrassing!"

"Okay, okay, girl," Brittany said, still laughing. "We're sorry."

"I'm not," Shaniqua said, still laughing.

Natasha stormed off. "I'm going into Macy's."

All three girls picked out clothes to try on from the junior's department.

"How do y'all like this?" Brittany asked dressed in a tan jean skirt that fell just above the knee with a matching top.

Shaniqua peeked her head out of the dressing room, "Uh, no. You need to show more skin, you ain't gonna catch nobody like that."

Brittany faced Natasha. "Does it make me look fat?"

"No," Natasha said, still annoyed.

Brittany stood in the mirror toying with her hair to take the focus off her body. She knew Natasha was just trying to be nice. At 5'5" and 150 pounds, Brittany knew she probably resembled a bulky, brown sack of potatoes.

A few moments later Shaniqua appeared,

dressed in a white spandex mini dress. "Oh yeah, Jordan will like this," she said twirling around in front of the mirror. "Y'all like?"

"Not!" Brittany shouted.

Shaniqua looked at Brittany as though she needed to be admitted to an asylum. "What?"

"Number one, it looks slutty, and two, the color is out of season. My mom said you're not supposed to wear white after Labor Day."

Shaniqua rolled her eyes. "It's not after Labor Day."

"It will be in a few days," Brittany said.

"Whatever, you're just jealous because you can't fit it," Shaniqua said.

"I wouldn't be caught dead in it," Brittany said, walking to Natasha's dressing room. "Tasha, how's your outfit?"

Natasha looked down at her bare wrists and then her bare ankles that should have been covered by the clothes she had on. "Short. Everything's too freakin' short."

"Well, I'm getting my outfit," Brittany said with confidence. She continued to study herself in the mirror. *If I could just lose ten pounds.*

"I'm getting mine, too," Shaniqua said.

"I thought you didn't have any money?" Brittany asked sarcastically.

"It's called the five-finger discount," Shaniqua whispered. "Nee Nee told me what to do. She said 'as long as it didn't have that alarm thing on it, it was fair game.' She said 'if you try to pull the

alarm thing off, ink would splatter on the clothes.'
I'm gonna to try it."

"Are you serious?" Natasha asked.

"Yeah, this dress doesn't have the alarm thing
on it."

Natasha's eyebrow curled up and the other,
down, creating a deep furrow across her forehead.
"Shaniqua, have you lost your mind? You can't do
that-- that's stealing."

"No duh," Shaniqua said indignantly.

"I swear, you had better not, Shaniqua. I'm not
kidding," Brittany pleaded, on the brink of tears.
"I'll get grounded for life if you get caught stealing.
I'll never be able to come to the mall again."

"It's not you doing anything, Brittany, it's me."

"Shaniqua, if you do that, you will not get a
ride home with us and your grandmother doesn't
have a car," Natasha said, returning to her dressing
room.

"So! I'll just call my cousin, Renee."

Natasha and Brittany hurriedly undressed.

Shaniqua watched her friends gather the
clothes they had tried on. "Y'all are so chicken. I
swear," she said, and then slammed the fitting room
door shut.

Moments later, Shaniqua emerged from the
dressing room, while her friends stood at the cash
register. Brittany and Natasha exchanged worried
looks. Then their eyes crept over the counter to the

cashier, a bubbly blond teen, who was completely unaware of the catastrophe that loomed in the air with the loud, hip music. Brittany dug around in her purse searching for money. Her hands were shaking. She glanced around the area for the police. There was none. She finally found her money in the side pocket of her Coach bag crammed underneath her many lipsticks. She paid the clerk, then nervously slid her hair behind her ear, waiting. Watching.

"I'll be out in the mall," Shaniqua said, walking past them with a smirk on her face.

Brittany and Natasha remained silent, pretending not to know Shaniqua. Tears welled up in Brittany's eyes while she waited for the cashier to give her change. The thought of what her dad would do to her when he found out made her cry. He always threatened her and her older brother that he had better not ever have to bail them out of jail. Her dad made it very clear that he had left that lifestyle a long time ago, and nothing was going to cast a shadow over his prominent career.
Natasha and Brittany steadily scanned the area for security while the clerk finished bagging the clothes.

"Thank you, come again," the cashier said cheerily.

Brittany grabbed her bag so quickly, she forgot to say 'Thank you'. Being polite was the last thing on her mind. "My dad's going to kill me."

"We'll explain to him that it wasn't our fault,"

Natasha said, storming pass Shaniqua in the mall as though she had never known her. "We'll tell him that she took it without our knowledge."

"Dang, how y'all just gone walk past me like that?" Shaniqua said, hurrying to catch up.

Natasha spun around, "Look, Shaniqua, I told you, you're not riding with us. We don't know you!"

"How you gone play me? You and I have been friends since the third grade, and now you don't know me?"

"I told you, if you stole that dress, that was it," Natasha said furiously.

"Dang girl, you ain't got to get your panties in a wad." Then Shaniqua let out a loud, obnoxious cackle.

Angrily, Brittany and Natasha started walking again.

"I didn't take it! Dang!"

Natasha and Brittany looked at each other with relief and let out nervous laughs while they waited for Shaniqua to catch up to them.

"I should kick your butt!" Natasha said, playfully swatting at Shaniqua.

Four o'clock couldn't come soon enough, Natasha thought. She had lost all desire to try on anything. Tall teenage girls had a hard enough time trying to find stylish clothes that fit, without having the added pressure of keeping a shopping companion from stealing. She swore if she ever made it out of Lenox without incident, Shaniqua would never be invited back to go shopping.

Chapter 3

Monday morning, the split of daylight seeped into Natasha's window, making her purple and white bedroom appear neon-like. She hated when she forgot to close her blinds the night before. It was a cruel way to wake up, especially when she still had twenty-eight minutes to sleep. She rested in bed letting her thoughts roam. *Stephen Perry.* Suddenly, Natasha sprang to life, leaping out of bed. She showered, dressed, and used the extra time to flat iron her hair; something she rarely did. Most days, she pulled her hair back into a smooth, low ponytail. Natasha checked herself over in the mirror. For once, her legs didn't resemble walking stilts. Satisfied, Natasha offered a tightlipped smile to the mirror and waited for her older brother Nate downstairs in the kitchen.

"Morning, Sweet Pea," Natasha's mom said, leaning over to kiss her on the forehead. "Don't you look cute this morning?"

Natasha wished her mom would find another

nickname for her. Sweet Pea had overstayed its welcome by at least seven years.

"Morning, Mom."

"You're down here early. You want some oatmeal?"

Natasha took a seat at the kitchen table. "No, thanks. I just cleaned my braces."

"Well, you can clean them again."

"No, Mom, I'll just have a glass of orange juice," Natasha pleaded. Her nerves were already in her stomach. There was no way she could eat anything this morning and expect to keep it down. She still had the butterflies from Saturday fluttering about. Natasha watched Nate stuff spoonfuls of cornflakes and milk in his mouth. "Are you ready?"

"Tasha, give your brother a chance to eat his breakfast. What are you so antsy about this morning?"

Natasha rolled her eyes behind her mother's back, and then noticed her art supplies scattered across the speckled brown granite countertop. "Oh, I almost forgot," she said, stowing them into her backpack. It would have been just her luck that she'd have to borrow supplies from Stephen Perry.

"Well, I've got a big day today," Natasha's mom said. "I'm closing that deal I've been working on all month."

Nate looked up. "Oh, the humongous house over in the Cascades?"

"Yes, finally. I thought that deal would never go down. That wife has to be the absolutely most demanding little old woman on the planet. There is nothing worse than a wannabe with new money. The house had to have this, but it can't have too much of that," she mimicked in a whiny voice. "Every room must be wired for an intercom and satellite radio. It's got to have a built-in toaster in the bathroom. Yadda, yadda, ya!"

Nate chuckled along with his mom.

Natasha was lost in her own world. Her mind was on getting out of art class. If only her dad hadn't told Mr. Arnold how excited she was to take his class, then bragged about how well she could draw.

Nate washed down his breakfast with a tall glass of orange juice and snagged a strawberry pop tart from the pantry. "Later, Mom."

Ms. Harris held open the kitchen door that led to the garage. "Have a good day. And remember-- "

"-- be pleasant in all that you do," Natasha cut in and recited in a monotone voice.

"That's my girl," Ms. Harris said, closing the door behind them.

Natasha shook her head. She swore her mother belonged in the Guinness Book of World Records for "Most Repetitious."

The second level of Miller Grove High was noisy as usual. Laughter, yelling, and metal lockers banging shut echoed through the hallways. Natasha was busy gathering her materials for her first three classes when Brittany strolled over, giggling.

"My my my, aren't we looking awfully purty this morning. Any special reason, huh, Mrs. Perry?" Brittany said, batting her eyelids.

Natasha smirked, thinking how Brittany had the most annoying little giggle. "No special reason. I woke up early, so I decided to flat iron my hair, if that's okay with you? And quit calling me Mrs. Perry."

"Uh-huh! So now, please tell the jury, was it clean or dirty hair that you flat ironed?" Brittany giggled.

Natasha frowned. "What?"

"If it was dirty hair, then in fact you didn't plan it. If the hair was clean, then you anticipated seeing a certain someone today and therefore took the necessary measures. Is that correct, Mrs. Perry?"

"Brittany, shut up."

"I rest my case. Mrs. Perry is indeed guilty of liking a certain someone by the name of Stephen Perry."

"Move, I'm going to homeroom," Natasha said, then slammed her locker shut and shoved pass Brittany.

Brittany giggled. "In a bit of a hurry to see Stephen Perry," she said with a British accent.

Natasha looked straight ahead, taking long strides, letting her walk say what her mouth would not. She knew saying anything would only add fuel to the already blazing fire. She was angry with her friends for creating this unnecessary strife in her life. Stephen Perry was no big deal. And to think about it, he wasn't even all that cute. In fact, he could pass for a first cousin with a banana, his skin tone matched perfectly. His eyes resembled little glassy, hazel marbles. He was about the same height that she was, which was a negative. He didn't play any sports, which meant he probably had little to no athletic ability. A negative. He wasn't popular. Definitely a negative.

Natasha turned down her homeroom corridor. There he was, just a few feet ahead of her. Her heart raced. Sweat pressed through the pores on her forehead. She walked into homeroom, her eyes glued to the floor. Definitely no eye contact. That way he couldn't draw a false, ridiculous conclusion about her liking him. She slid into her seat and kept her eyes on her desk, praying that Ms. Andrews would not call on her for foolishness, like passing out the weekly lunch menu.

Finally, the bell ended homeroom.

Thank you, Jesus! Natasha sat there for a while, patiently waiting for all the students to leave the room. She watched Stephen huddled in with the other students through the doorway. She gathered her belongings and headed out, too.

"What's up Natasha?" Stephen said, leaning against the wall right outside the doorway.

Natasha jumped. Her knees were wobbly, and threatening to buckle from under her. "You scared me," Natasha said, placing her hand over her racing heart.

"Sorry. I just thought we could walk to class together. Since we've got to walk all the way to the other side of campus, might as well have some company."

Natasha offered a weak smile.

"That is, unless you have some other plans."

"No." Natasha was angry with herself. This ugly boy had too much power over her. She couldn't seem to give more than one-word answers.

Stephen smiled. "Cool."

His smile was infectious. Natasha found herself smiling because he smiled. She liked his teeth. A positive.

"Were you able to find all the supplies that we need for class?" Stephen asked.

"Pretty much."

"Well, whatever you didn't get, I'm sure I have several."

Natasha's eyes darted between Stephen and the hallways. She was on the lookout for her friends. If they saw her, she'd never be able to live it down.

"Really?" Natasha asked.

"Yeah, I've been drawing since I was five years old. I mean studying. This art class is really just an easy 'A' for me."

Natasha's eyes rested on the peach fuzz above his lip. "You must be pretty good then?"

"I'm okay. I hope to be able to make a living at it some day. You know, bypass the whole 'starving artist thing.'"

Ms. Thang

They laughed and continued weaving in and out of conversations easily. Natasha listened as he talked about different works of art that he had created or seen. She had only studied art since middle school. It was refreshing to have someone interested in the same subject. She relaxed into the feeling of friendship, and drank in his knowledge, happy to have made a new friend.

Chapter 4

Shaniqua felt herself growing fonder of Jordan Kelley with each passing day. For weeks, they stole stares and caught glances from one another. She marveled at how he would stroll in homeroom, mostly late, wearing baggy jeans, a designer shirt and Timberlands, if he showed up at all. And when he did come, he never carried books, but kept a pencil tucked neatly behind his ear to accent his huge diamond-like studs. He wore his hair corn rolled straight back which revealed his nicely chiseled bone structure. His skin tone matched the bark of a Georgia live oak tree. His limbs were slim like the tree's branches. He was average height, with a scrawny build that even loose-fitting attire failed to camouflage. But Jordan Kelley was the epitome of cool; at the ripe age of sixteen, he had already mastered the black man's pimp stroll.

Homecoming was only two weeks away and Shaniqua was beginning to wonder if Jordan would ever make a move. She sat anxiously in homeroom, feeling the weight of Jordan's heavy stare as they sat parallel to one another in the back of the room. Shaniqua could see that Jordan was definitely biting the bait on her line, and she was going to reel him in like the prize fish that he was.

She studied the clock. She had four minutes to make her move. She nibbled on her fingernail while watching Mrs. Roberson, debating if she should attempt it. Mrs. Roberson could turn evil in an instant if she even sensed someone was doing something against school policy. Everyone thought she was mean because she had been cheated out of having both chin and neck. Instead, she was given a nice, smooth ski slope that went from her bottom lip downhill to her chest. Shaniqua discreetly surveyed the classroom. Mrs. Roberson was busy reading something. Time ticked, two minutes down. Immobilized, she stared at the brown, commercial grade carpet. Her heart began pounding so fast and loud, she wondered if the nearby students could hear it. Another minute passed before she located her red notebook with Jordan's named doodled all over it, the unconscious embroidery of love. Her fingers trembled as she ripped out a sheet of paper and wrote:

Dear Jordan,

I know you don't know me, but I was wondering if you have a girlfriend. If yes, I understand. But if no, I was hoping maybe we could get together. My number is 404-555-1212.

Peace,

Shaniqua Williams

She folded the letter into a little paper football and passed it over two rows. The bell rang ending homeroom.

When Shaniqua returned home from school, her grandmother was in the kitchen as usual preparing dinner for the two of them and any other family member who happened to stop by.

"How was school?" Her grandmother said, standing at the kitchen sink with her back toward Shaniqua.

Shaniqua took a seat at the oak table that was twice her age. "Fine, Granny."

"You got homework?"

"No, ma'am."

Granny turned to look at the granddaughter she had been raising since birth. She studied her. And then moved closer to Shaniqua to get a better view. The green and white checkered linoleum crackled with each step. "Chile, what in the world you got on?"

"Nee Nee loaned it to me."

Granny shook her head, but her salt and pepper curls, too tight to move, stayed in place. "That girl ain't got the brains of a Betsey bug; you don't wanna follow in her footsteps."

"I'm not following in her footsteps, Granny, you just being old-fashion," Shaniqua said, teasing. But she knew her grandmother meant business.

Granny placed her hand on her round hip. "Call it ol' fashion if you want to, but times ain't changed that much, you looking like some ol' street woman. You ain't but fifteen and as far as I'm concerned, still crawlin' backwards. Ya hear?"

"Yes, ma'am."

"Lawd, Jesus," Granny said, still shaking her head and mumbling under her breath. She made it clear on several occasions that she had raised her four kids already and that she wasn't up for no foolishness with a youngster still wet behind the ears.

The phone rang.

"I'll get it," Shaniqua said, and darted upstairs to her bedroom, "Hello."

"Is Shaniqua there?"

"This her," Shaniqua said staring at an old Bow Wow poster.

"What's up Shorty Red? This Jordan."

Shaniqua's heart quickened. Jordan Kelley's voice was deep, not Barry White deep, but deep to be only sixteen. Most boys in her class had high-pitched voices. She never really heard his voice in homeroom because he was always quiet and when he did talk, it was low. "Hi, Jordan, what's up?"

"You."

Shaniqua's smile spread from cheek to cheek. "So you got my note?" *Stupid question. He would've never called if he didn't get the note.*

"Who's on the phone?" Granny yelled.

"It's for me!"

"That's your moms?" Jordan asked.

"No, my grandmother. I live with her."

"Damn Shorty, you were off the chain today!"

She giggled. "For real?"

"Yeah! So when can we hook up?"

"I don't know."

"How 'bout tomorrow?"

"Okay, where you wanna meet?"

"Meet me at my ol' school."

"What old school?"

"My ride ... it's a blue '68 Impala, it'll be parked on Covington Street tomorrow morning before school."

"Okay."

"All right, Shorty, I'll holla!"

"Bye," Shaniqua said softly, fighting hard to contain her excitement. Her cousin Nee Nee's plan was coming together. She laid on the bed, hugging her pillow, looking up at the dusty ceiling that should have been painted several lease renewals ago. She was definitely on her way to becoming an 'It' girl. She was finally going to experience love, and with the hottest boy in the school. Tomorrow couldn't come soon enough. She leaped off the bed and began jumping up and down, doing strange, funny dances in the mirror, chanting, "Go girl, go girl, go girl!"

Then she rushed to dial Nee Nee's number; she was definitely going to need another outfit. Granny didn't have money to buy her a lot of clothes; they were barely surviving off of her social security check each month, which is why they stayed in their cramped two-bedroom townhouse for the last ten years.

"Hello?" Nee Nee said.

"Who's your girl, who's your girl!"

"What's up, Shaniqua, I'm tryin' to get ready for work."

"The plan is working!" Shaniqua shouted. "I'm meeting Jordan Kelley tomorrow morning. I'm so happy."

"See, I told you."

"But, I need an outfit."

"No problem, I'll bring something down there on my way to work."

"No, you can't. Granny's starting to trip about my gear. I'll stop by in the morning on my way to school."

"The club doesn't close until seven a.m., so I'll just be getting home. Do not wake me up, Shaniqua! I'll let momma know I'm leaving a couple of outfits on the couch for you."

Shaniqua hung up the phone feeling excited. She glanced around her room. She had so many posters plastered on the walls, the eggshell paint was barely visible. Her eyes rested on a crumpled up Omarion poster. She smiled, because Jordan was her Omarion. She loved it when a plan came together. She smiled into the mirror, admiring her reflection. Her braids were still neat. She inched closer to the mirror to give her skin a thorough check. It was definitely time to spread the mint green mask on her face. Red bumps shined more on fairer complexions. No one knew where her light skin came from; most of her mother's family was dark. No one ever talked much about her mother and definitely not her father. They were as much of a mystery to her today as they had been all her life. Her mother, Karen, would occasionally show up every few years to dry out from drinking. They would hug like distant relatives and part ways whenever Karen got the taste again. And the times when her mother did stick around for a spell, they didn't talk much. Karen spent most of her time listening to Granny's sermons and then when Karen couldn't take it anymore, Shaniqua would hear her mother yell, "Well, you didn't say anything to daddy!" and slam the door shut, leaving until the next time.

Chapter 5

The following morning, Shaniqua made sure she popped in the hazel-colored contacts Nee Nee had given her over the summer break. She slipped on a gray sweat suit and gym shoes and ran two blocks down the street to her Aunt Kathy's apartment to borrow her cousin's clothes. Shaniqua dressed quickly in a red mini skirt, white top and white high-heels. She tiptoed into the bathroom, brushed on black mascara to straighten out her curly lashes, and then dabbed on some reddish lipstick. She closed her aunt's front door quietly and headed to the bus stop.

When Shaniqua stepped up on the bus, she heard whistling. She kept her chin tucked into her chest.

"Hey, hey girl, you in the red skirt, come back here," a boy yelled from the back of the bus.

"Naw, man, you ain't got nothing for her. I got something for her little ass."

Shaniqua took a seat in the third row from the front next to Lucy Looty Booty. She sat down carefully, trying not to disturb her. If Shaniqua hadn't been so afraid to go to the back of the bus, she would have never sat next to Lucy. She was one of the meanest girls in the school. Behind Lucy's back, everyone called her Lucy Looty Booty because of her big bubble butt. She would fight anyone who said anything to her face, boys and girls alike.

"Damn girl, you look like you working at a strip club," Lucy said in a deep, scruffy voice.

If Shaniqua hadn't known better, she would have mistaken her for an ugly boy. Shaniqua gave a nervous smile, then dug around in her book bag as a distraction. She wasn't about to get into verbal combat with Lucy. She was tall and big, and could crush her to death just by sitting on her.

When Shaniqua finally arrived at school, she made her way to Covington Street. She wondered why Jordan elected not to park in the student parking lot. She could see his silhouette in the car from afar. She felt awkward as she approached, as though she could no longer walk in her three-inch heels. Her knees felt knobbier than usual, and her toes seem to point inward, pigeon like. She opened the car door and sat down on his torn leather seat for a chance to chat before school started.

Jordan was stretched out in his seat, his hand poised over his groin with an I-know-I'm-cool grin. "Damn, Shorty Red, you doin' it!" he said, looking Shaniqua up and down.

Shorty Red was a term that some southern boys coined for light-skinned females. It was as common as girl. But somehow Jordan saying it sounded sweet. She smiled at the compliment; her nerves had temporarily silenced her voice. "Thank you," she strained softly, still trying to digest that she was actually sitting face to face with Jordan Kelley in his car.

"Loosen up, girl, I ain't gonna bite you."

Shaniqua laughed away the nervous tension.

"I like your eyes."

Shaniqua smiled bashfully. "Thank you."

Jordan pulled his black Atlanta Braves baseball cap snug over his brows. "So what's up, what you wanna do?"

"When?"

"Now, you here, ain't you?"

"Yeah."

"Shit, let's kick it."

"You mean skip school?"

"What, you scared?"

"No, but what happens if they call my grandmother?"

"They ain't gonna call your house. Tomorrow, write an excuse and give it to Mrs. Roberson."

Shaniqua sat there quietly trying to decide if she should trust what he says. She always heard of people skipping school, but she hadn't known anyone brave enough to do it except her cousin Nee Nee, and that was a few years ago. Well, actually, now that she thought about it, Nee Nee didn't have to skip. Her mother didn't care if she went or not.

And eventually when she got into the eleventh grade, she stopped going altogether.

"All right," Shaniqua said, though not totally convinced. Then she remembered her plan to become an 'It' girl and get one of the most popular boys in school. *Definitely necessary!* "So where are we going?"

Jordan turned his cap backwards and cranked up the car. "We'll ride around for a minute, maybe down by the AUC?"

"What's the AUC?"

"Atlanta University Center, where Clark, Morehouse and Spelman is."

"I always wanted to go down there for the step shows, but never had a ride."

"Let's check it out, my cousin goes to Clark."

They rode down to Southwest Atlanta, listening to the latest rap music. They turned down James P. Brawley Drive and watched the sharply dressed college students stroll the promenade.

"When I graduate, I'm coming here," Shaniqua said. Though she hadn't ever thought of going to a four-year college, she always knew she wanted to pursue cosmetology.

"So what you wanna do now?" Jordan asked.

"I don't care."

"Let's go by my cousin's crib two blocks over."

"Okay."

They entered an old, small shotgun house.

Though it was dimly lit, Shaniqua could see the shapes of liquor bottles strewn across the countertops, along with empty beer cans and pizza boxes. Two broken barstools held the wall. The old sagging brown couch looked as though something unidentifiable would come crawling out of it any moment.

Shaniqua turned up her nose. "Who'd you say live here again?"

"My cousin, well, actually he's my play cousin. I've known Lance since I was six years old; he's from my neighborhood. He gave me a key and said I could come down and chill out here anytime I want."

"Is he here?"

"Probably not, he's always by some freak's, I mean girl's house. His roommate is probably here though. Wait here for a minute, let me check it out."

Jordan grabbed his groin and strolled down the narrow hallway that ran from the front of the house all the way to the back. Both bedroom doors were open and the rooms empty. Jordan turned around and yelled down the hall. "It's cool. Let's chill in my cousin's bedroom, he's got a bunch of movies and Playstation."

Shaniqua started down the hallway. She could tell this was definitely a bachelor's pad. Only boys would stay here. The crumbling walls were desperate for a fresh coat of paint, the bathroom looked like it hadn't been cleaned since the house was built in the early 1900's, while floorboards creaked and shifted with each step.

Jordan turned on the television, then the video game. "Do you play?"

"No, not really."

"I'm going to play for a minute, cool?"

"Yeah."

Jordan played basketball, while Shaniqua sat on the frameless bed pretending to be interested. Her eyes were on the TV screen, but her mind was still on the fact that she had actually skipped school. Somehow, it didn't feel so fun. She felt like she was missing out on something at school. But she went along, because Jordan was cool and this was what the cool kids did, she thought. Secretly, she was still hoping the school wasn't calling her house. Her eyes combed every inch of the room. Clothes and dirty underwear were the rugs for the worn out hardwood floor. Dust offered a protective coating over everything. Empty bottles and cups sat on the milk crate next to the bed. Papers and unsharpened pencils where strewn across an old dresser. The only things that looked cared for in the room were the 36" TV and a top-of-the-line stereo system next to it.

"My fault, Shorty Red, let me turn this off," Jordan said, reaching for the game. "Damn girl, you fine as hell."

Shaniqua blushed, forgetting about how bored she had been watching him play for the last hour and a half.

Jordan pulled off his cap and set it on the milk crate. "Get comfortable, you can take off your shoes if you want. We're gonna chill out here for the rest of the day. Come on over here, I ain't gone bite you."

Shaniqua grinned. Then moved closer to where Jordan was sitting on the bed. His scent filled her nostrils. It was a popular scent, but she couldn't determine which one. It smelled sexy, masculine yet sweet. Her lips parted into a smile. She was smiling so hard and unsophisticatedly that her cheeks burned. She wanted to tell him to rush her to the emergency room, her body temperature had risen twenty-five degrees.

"So what's up with us?" Jordan said, caressing Shaniqua's hand.

"What you want to be up?" She said still smiling, but not making eye contact. Instead, she kept her eyes glued to the scratched planks in the floor.

"You tryin' to be down with me?"

"Yeah."

"So how we gonna make this official?"

"I don't know."

"Do I get to kiss my new girlfriend or what?"

Shaniqua blushed, "I guess."

Jordan gently turned Shaniqua's face toward his. Then Shaniqua felt Jordan lips meet hers. Beads of perspiration quickly swelled on her back and chest. She closed her eyes and tried not to smile through the kiss, but she was happy that she had gotten one of the finest boys in the school to be her boyfriend. Jordan began exploring her body with very sure, very skillful hands. Shaniqua's heart was pounding, her emotions swirling. She was nervous, scared, but his touch felt good, yet uncomfortable. Then Jordan reached to pull her skirt down. Shaniqua shook her head, but Jordan kept tugging at it. She grabbed his hand to stop him, but he swiftly employed his other hand and worked her skirt down past her knees.

Shaniqua pulled away from him. "What are you doing?" she asked, struggling to pull her skirt back up.

"You like it?"

"No ... yes ... I mean I ain't ready for this."

"You ain't ready. What, you don't like me?"

"Yeah."

"Well, if you like me, then show me," Jordan said, inching her skirt back down.

Shaniqua searched his eyes, and then looked away. She didn't know that being with him meant doing the nasty. She had heard other kids were having sex, but she had planned to wait at least until she was madly in love. The pressure was on. Her thoughts raced over her Christian principals to abstain. She wondered if all the gawking at her in homeroom meant he was in love with her. I guess this is it. Shaniqua gazed into his eyes, silently pledging her heart.

Jordan accepted the nonverbal affirmation. He stood up and unclamped his belt, letting his baggy jeans fall to the floor in one swift motion. He laid down on top of her and began kissing her on the neck.

Shaniqua tried to relax and enjoy the moment, though it didn't feel so good. Sex was painful. It was nothing like how she envisioned her first time would be. She always thought that she would look into her lover's eyes and he would tell her how much he loved her and needed her and how they'd spend the rest of their lives together, like they did in the movies. Instead, it was rigid and fast, no long, slow tongue kisses or "I love you." Even his cologne no longer smelled good. She kept her thoughts on more pleasant things, like how she had a new man and she was definitely going to be an 'It' girl now. Shaniqua lay there, thankful that it was over after a couple of minutes.

"How you feel, Shorty?" Jordan asked, pulling his body away from hers.

Shaniqua offered a weak smile, almost near tears.

Jordan studied her face. "Don't cry. It'll be better next time. I promise."

She closed her eyes, letting his words fill her. She snuggled sweetly into him like bees in a hive, satisfied that Jordan appreciated her gift to him.

"I'm hungry," Shaniqua said softly, sweeping a couple of micro braids behind her ear. She had seen Brittany do it at least a million times.

Abruptly, he withdrew his embrace and headed for the shower. "Can't, we gotta go."

Shaniqua reclaimed the gym clothes she had left earlier that morning at Nee Nee's house and returned home, conscious of the blue and black bruises on her neck. She liked the passion marks because it was a reminder that she wasn't dreaming. It was real. She was officially Jordan Kelley's girlfriend and had the evidence to prove it. Her only problem would be hiding them from her grandmother. She knew Granny would kill her not once, but ten times over, if she knew all that she had done that day. But it was her secret, her memory, and her special beginning with her first love. And she planned to love him as a cactus does dry heat.

Chapter 6

Shaniqua entered school proud as a peacock. Her hickeys were her feathers. With her back arched, shoulders upright, allowing her swaying narrow hips to be the main attraction, she strutted through the halls the way popular girls did. She felt different. And today would be different. She would be an 'It' girl that the boys walked to class and everyone envied. She would have someone to smooch with in the corners before, during, and after school. But most of all, she'd being going to her first homecoming dance with Jordan Kelley.

Shaniqua posted up against her locker, then slid a fresh piece of mint gum in her mouth, stalling, waiting for Jordan to come and walk her to homeroom.

Natasha walked over. "Hey girl, where were you yesterday?"

Brittany interrupted. "Oh, she got a hickey!"

Shaniqua beamed, conceitedly.

"Let me see," Natasha said, turning Shaniqua's

chin. "Dang girl, did you have a fight with a vampire?"

Brittany shook her head in disbelief. "Who gave you all those hickeys?"

"My man, who else?"

Brittany turned up her nose. "And who is that?"

Shaniqua winked and offered a slow and informed smile. "Jordan Kelley. I told y'all I was going to make him mine and I did yesterday."

Natasha squealed. "Girl, tell us what happened?"

Then suddenly, the bell interrupted.

"Gotta go, we'll finish at lunch," Shaniqua said as she dashed off.

They watched her nearly run down the hallway.

Shaniqua strolled into homeroom looking especially cute, her braids gathered into a high ponytail, revealing large hoop earrings that gently brushed her shoulders. Dressed in tight jeans and a little black and white top with a low V-cut in the front, she hoped that she wouldn't be sent home for exposing her midriff. Granny would be all over her like white on rice. She took her seat just as Jordan walked in. Her cheeks burned with happiness. She waited for him to make eye contact. He didn't. He was busy chatting with Rick and James.

The tardy bell rang, prompting Mrs. Roberson to begin homeroom activities. "Good morning, when I call your name, please raise your hand."

Shaniqua stole a quick peek at Jordan. He was looking at something on his desk. She ripped out a sheet of notebook paper and discreetly began writing:

Dear Jordan,

I waited for you to call last night. I guess you must have gotten busy. I succeeded in hiding the hickeys from my grandmother. Thank goodness (smile). Let's talk after class. I just wanted to drop this note to let you know I was thinking about you, sexy pie.

Hugs and kisses,

Your girl, Shaniqua

She handed the note to Cindy, who then passed it to Rick. Rick and James exchanged knowing glances and chuckled.

Mrs. Roberson rose from her desk, her ski slope jiggled. "Excuse me gentlemen, but what is it that's so funny? Perhaps you care to delight the rest of your classmates. Rick? James?"

"No, ma'am," James said.

Rick shook his head, the note clenched in his fist.

Still peering suspiciously over her silver, thin-rimmed glasses, Mrs. Roberson sat down and resumed roll call.

Rick slid the note to Jordan. Minutes later, the bell rang ending homeroom. Jordan rushed out of the classroom.

"Jordan, wait up!" she shouted, trying to catch him, but he already turned down another corridor. Her first hour class was in the opposite direction, so she decided to meet up with him later.

When the bell rang to begin fourth hour lunch, Shaniqua shoved her books into her locker and hurried down the hallway that housed Jordan's locker. For the first three periods, she couldn't take her mind off him. Now she would finally have a moment to be with him. As she approached, she saw Jordan leaning against his locker, talking to a girl from the eleventh grade. Shaniqua had seen him with her several times before. Cherise was one of the popular girls, president of the pep club. She was always at the basketball and football games, leading chants and cheers. Somehow her voice could always be heard through the thunderous crowd.

"Hi, Cherise," Shaniqua said, though grinning at Jordan.

Cherise turned up her nose and mouth into a sour smile.

"Hi, Jordan," Shaniqua chimed, while her eyes danced, and her heart did somersaults.

"What's up?" Jordan said, then turned his attention back to Cherise.

"You got a moment?" Shaniqua said softly.

Jordan scowled. "Can't you see I'm busy?"

Shaniqua stood there with her mouth hanging open, devastated, then turned and walked away.

She heard Cherise say, "Who in the hell is that bitch?"

"Nobody," Jordan said.

Everything in her body wanted to run back there and bang the loudmouth heffa's head against

Jordan's locker. Better yet, she could bite Cherise, since her skin tone and texture was comparable to a Nestle Crunch candy bar. But Shaniqua had to be realistic about her physical capabilities. She was only 5'2" and weighed 105 pounds. Both Cherise and Jordan towered over her. She quietly meandered her way to the cafeteria to meet her friends, wondering why Jordan was being so cold.

Natasha's long arms waved in the air. "Hurry up, girl, come on over here."

Shaniqua placed her lunch tray on the table. "What's up, y'all?"

"You tell us, Ms. Thang," Brittany chimed.

Shaniqua playfully fanned herself. "Dang, can a sista breathe?"

"Nope!" Brittany and Natasha said in unison, giggling and slapping high-fives.

Shaniqua blushed. "Okay. It all started when I sent Jordan a letter asking if he had a girlfriend and to call if he didn't. When he called my house, we agreed to hook up the next morning before school. I met him at his car, we talked for awhile, but there wasn't enough time, so we decided to skip school."

"Oh my God, Shaniqua, you skipped school with him?" Brittany asked.

"You know it."

Natasha's brows puckered. "And the school didn't call your house?"

"Nope. This morning, I gave Mrs. Roberson a fake note excusing me for yesterday. And that was it."

"Girl, weren't you scared of getting caught?" Brittany asked.

"Scared of what?"

"My dad would kill me dead."

"Mine too," Natasha said.

Shaniqua ignored their comments and continued over the noisy lunchroom buzz, "We hung out at his cousin's house down by the AUC. It was cool. Then guess what happened."

"What?" they said.

"Jordan asked me to be his girl."

"His girl?" Brittany's face scrunched into a frown. "I heard he was going out with Cherise Evans."

"Well, not anymore," Shaniqua said, slapping high-fives with Natasha.

"So, Jordan Kelley gave you all those hickeys?" Brittany asked indignantly.

"Of course," Shaniqua said, proudly sporting her new badges of coupling. "And now I've got someone to take me to the homecoming dance. I told y'all I was going to work it, didn't I?"

"Yeah, you did it, girlfriend," Natasha said.

"If I were you, I wouldn't let someone suck all on me like that. It looks very slutty," Brittany said, still frowning.

"Well, you ain't me, and I ain't you," Shaniqua said with a smirk and began eating her lunch. "Sounds to me like somebody's been sipping on Hateorade!"

Brittany stuffed a few chips in her mouth. "Please, don't flatter yourself."

Natasha scanned the lunchroom. "So, where is Jordan now? For some reason I thought he had fourth hour lunch, too."

Shaniqua's eyes fell on her chicken sandwich.

"Girl, please, Jordan takes fourth, fifth and sixth," Brittany said.

Shaniqua shrugged her shoulders and picked up her sandwich, though she didn't have a taste for it. If she ate, then she wouldn't have to talk. She raked her fork through the instant mashed potatoes. There was no way she could get them down. Granny's homemade garlic mashed potatoes had spoiled her. The bell sounded, relieving Shaniqua of finishing her lunch.

Algebra, the last class of the day, couldn't end soon enough. Shaniqua sat anxiously watching the clock, passing minutes like hours, barely paying attention. Exponentials could wait. Her love life was more important. She gazed out the window and into the commons area, fantasizing how Jordan was going to be waiting for her by her locker after school. Then, he would wrap her in his arms and plant sweet kisses on her neck, cheeks, and lips. Next, she would get into his car with the rest of his friends for a ride home.

Finally, the bell signified the end of the school day. Shaniqua fumbled around in her locker, waiting for Jordan. Several minutes later, she scurried around to his locker, but there was no sign of him. She leaped down the stairs like Marion Jones and hurried outside to scan the student parking lot for his car. She saw it—big, old, and barely blue. There were a few people standing around Jordan's car, her new friends. She looked closer. Her heart pounded. Her new enemy. Cherise was laughing. Shaniqua stared at her thinking, that when she snaps her jaws back in a laugh, a poppa alligator ain't got nothing on her. Shaniqua contemplated walking over to the car, but she really didn't want any more confrontations with the loudmouth of the South. She wasn't quite sure how long she'd be able to refrain from intertwining her fingers in her orange-blond hair that was much too light for her complexion. Cherise and her friends piled into Jordan's car, then he peeled off, burning rubber. Shaniqua watched the car race down the street until she could no longer see it and headed for her bus. Her heart was heavy; love didn't feel so good at the moment.

When Shaniqua arrived home from school, she immediately began phoning Jordan's house. She had spoken to his mother more times than she dare count. Then around 8:30 p.m., her phone rang.

"Hello."

"Shaniqua there?"

She smiled, quickly forgetting how angry she had been earlier. "This me."

"My mom's pissed. Don't call my house like that again!"

"I'm sorry, Jordan, I didn't mean ..."

"What do you want?"

"I was calling to talk since we didn't get a chance to at school today."

"What we got to talk about?"

"Well, uh, nothing in particular. I just thought we were going to hang out some at school."

"I don't get down like that."

"What do you mean?"

"I don't hang out with chicks like that."

"You hung out with Cherise after school."

"I gotta go, I'll holla," he said and slammed the phone down.

Sitting statue-still, Shaniqua could hardly believe what she had witnessed. He was such a different person from the day before. Yesterday, he had been so kind. She had felt so close to him while they stretched out face to face in the bed. They had been together in a way that was certain and concrete. Yet today, that feeling was fleeting, leaving emptiness to roam in her stomach. She was hurting. *Is this how love feels?*

Chapter 7

The next morning in homeroom, Shaniqua dared to look at Jordan. Approaching him was becoming more complicated with each passing day. She scribbled her thoughts on paper.

Dear Jordan,

What's up? What's going on between us? Have your feelings for me changed? Or are you just going through some other issues? I know we haven't discussed this before, but are we going to the homecoming dance together?

Hugs and kisses,

Your girl, Shaniqua

With her special communication team in place, Shaniqua nodded to Cindy to get her attention. But Cindy goofily stared off into space as though she was telepathically connected to aliens. Shaniqua looked two rows over to Rick. His cheesy grin showed he was ready. Shaniqua peeked at Mrs. Roberson sitting at her desk with her head bent reading, and then looked at Cindy again. She discreetly waved her hand to get Cindy's attention. The freckles on Cindy's face spread into an eager-to-please smile. She was sweet like the color of her strawberry hair, but quiet like most nerds. Shaniqua nodded, it was time, and then handed the note off to Cindy. When Cindy passed the note to Rick, he handed her another one. In Cindy's overzealous quest to be a part of something devious, she overthrew the letter to Shaniqua, causing it to go sailing through the air like a tiny white kite with thin blue lines. Shaniqua quickly knocked her pencil to the floor, so that she'd have an excuse to get up. She eased the wide part of her stiletto on top of the note before Mrs. Roberson saw it and casually picked up her pencil. She slid the note across the floor with as much tenacity as a hockey player guides an ice puck, ready to score. Nothing would keep her from her goal of reading Jordan's note.

As soon as the bell rang, Jordan leaped from his seat and was the first one out of the classroom. With the note clenched tightly in her hand, Shaniqua started down the corridor. Curiosity was overtaking her. She stopped abruptly and stood off to the side so the other students could pass easily. She drew in a deep breath to calm her nerves and steady her fingers, then unfolded the letter:

What's up Shaniqua? You were looking fine today. When can we skip school? Call me. 404.555.1414. Rick

Rick? "Ueww!" Shaniqua balled up the letter

with lightning speed and rammed it in the trashcan, causing the bang of the metal flap to echo through the hall as she hurried to U.S. history class.

The posse gathered at their usual lunch table.

"Girl, what's wrong with you?" Natasha asked, watching Shaniqua place her lunch tray on the table slowly. "What are you down in the dumps about?"

"Nothing."

"Shaniqua, don't even try it. What's up?" Natasha said.

Shaniqua looked at Natasha and then Brittany, deciding whether to trust them with her issues. Being an only child, she had mastered the art of keeping her feelings private. She really wasn't up for Brittany's sarcasm or Natasha's lectures. But she needed help in the worst way. "It's Jordan. He's been acting real funny toward me."

"Funny how?" Brittany said, sweeping her hair behind her ear.

The clinking of metal forks and spoons colliding with hard plastic food trays resonated in Shaniqua's ears. "He's not talking to me. He won't even look my way in homeroom."

"Girl, you know some brothas don't want people in their business at school," Natasha said. "They try to act as if they don't like the girl. You know, trying to be cool."

Brittany pursed her lips. "Oh, really? He sure doesn't act like that with Cherise. Her locker is down the hall from mine, and he's always up in her face."

Shaniqua toyed with the applesauce on her tray.

"How does he act when you guys are alone?" Natasha asked.

"The day we hooked up, everything was cool. He was nice to me. But ever since then, he hasn't talked to me. I called him last night and he got mad and then hung up."

"Sounds to me like he's ... not trying to be with you. What happened when you all hooked up? Did y'all do the nasty or something?" Brittany said.

Natasha frowned. "Brittany please, of course they didn't, she's not that stupid."

Shaniqua kept her eyes low, steadfast on her food. Her hamburger looked disgusting, all shriveled up on a gigantic bun. The tatter tots had dried out and the green beans looked like they could come alive any moment and slither their slimy green selves around her neck and strangle her.

"Tasha, let Shaniqua speak for herself," Brittany scolded.

"Well, did you?" Natasha asked.

Shaniqua's lips quivered, but she couldn't speak. She nodded her head.

"No, you didn't!" Brittany squealed, as if she was amused.

Natasha shook her head. "Shaniqua, how could you?"

Shaniqua shrugged her shoulders.

"We told you Jordan wasn't about anything," Natasha said.

Brittany was shaking her head vigorously back and fourth. "Girl, he played you big time. He had only one thing on his mind. And from the looks of it, he probably never even broke up with Cherise."

"Dang Brittany, can't you see the girl is hurt enough," Natasha said looking at Brittany, then turned her attention back to Shaniqua. "Why'd you do it?"

"'Cause he wanted to. He said we were gonna be a couple."

Brittany giggled. "Sista girl, uh, buddy played you for real."

"No, he didn't, he's just going through something," Shaniqua protested.

"Well, it can't be that serious, he's always smiling up in Cherise's face."

"Brittany, please," Natasha said. "Give her a break. We don't really know what's going on."

"Maybe y'all don't, but I do. She got played. All he wanted was the B-O-O-T-Y and she gave it up. And now he doesn't want anything to do with her."

Natasha shot Brittany a look that could have decapitated her had her eyes been two knives. Brittany was cool most times, but that Goody-two-shoes-wearing saint was on her last nerve today.

Brittany flung her hair back and huddled close to Shaniqua. "Well, at least tell us what it feels like," she whispered.

Shaniqua was in no mood to give them a play by play, but since she was the first in the group to have sex, she owed them. She wondered if she should tell the truth or lie like all the other girls and say how great it was. Her voice was barely audible. "It's not all that. Really, it hurt. We only did it for like maybe two minutes, then he started groaning and having these spasms and then it was over. I was glad, too. When we got up, I was bleeding. I cleaned myself up and he dropped me off."

Brittany scrunched up her face. "Just like that?"

Shaniqua nodded.

Brittany was shaking her head with a smug look on her face. If she lifted her head any higher, her nose would rub the ceiling. "Girl, please, I would never let a dude handle me like that."

"Like what?" Shaniqua said.

"The way Jordan handled you. He didn't love you or care anything about you. He only wanted the booty."

A cloud of silence hung in the air, while a downpour of noise surrounded them. Most students were in groups, laughing, talking, eating and poking fun at other students. The lights reflected on the pale yellow walls, casting a peaceful amber glow on everyone. All three girls seemed to be lost in their own muddled thoughts, pondering what they would have done.

"Shoot, I have too much self pride to let somebody take advantage of me like that," Brittany said, combing her fingers through her hair.

"My mother said, 'You have to love yourself enough, otherwise people will run over you.' And Brittany Ann Brown ain't going out like a sucka for no brotha!"

"I agree, Brittany, but do you have to be so crass?" Natasha shot back, trying to ease Shaniqua's pain. She truly felt sorry that her best friend was so clueless to the game that brothers played.

Brittany rolled her eyes heavenward. "Well, Tasha, would you have done it with him?"

"No, of course not, my brother has already hipped me to the game. Nate said, 'Boys are only after one thing right now and they are going to get it from whichever girl they can and then go on to the next.' He said, I don't have to worry about them trying that with me because they know him. He said, they try the weak-minded, fast girls, that don't have brothers," Natasha said to Brittany.

"Yep, that's pretty much the same thing my brother, Kevin, told me."

Then Natasha turned her attention back to Shaniqua. Her bony shoulders were slumped forward. Her head was hanging so low her braids amused themselves in her food. Natasha realized that she had done no better than Brittany had. Natasha's voice softened. "Shaniqua, you really should have talked with someone older and more experienced before you went with him."

"I did, my cousin, Renee."

Brittany flashed a sarcastic smirk. "Oh, and

what is it that she does for a living, shake her ass for money? Uh-huh, real good, Shaniqua, real good."

"Brittany, shut up!" Natasha said.

Brittany bit into her burger while Shaniqua's eyes filled with hot, angry tears. She was angry with her sorry-ass parents, angry for not having any siblings, angry that she didn't have anyone in her life to help her, to coach her through like her friends had. All she had was Granny, and Granny was too old and set in her Jurassic ways.

Natasha rubbed Shaniqua's back. "Girl, it's not the end of the world, but if I were you, I wouldn't contact Jordan anymore. If he wants to be with you, he'll call you," Natasha said. "And definitely don't do the nasty with him anymore."

"What about homecoming?" Shaniqua said.

"What about it? It's not that big of a deal if you don't have a date."

"Easy for you to say, you'll be going with Stephen," Shaniqua said.

"No, I'm not. I keep telling you guys, Stephen and I are just friends. That's it."

"But this was supposed to be the year we went to everything," Shaniqua said.

"Girl, we are only sophomores, it's not the end of our lives," Natasha replied.

Brittany clapped her hands together. "I've got an excellent idea. Why don't we all go together and just hang out. That way my parents will probably let me go."

"I don't want to go with a bunch of girls. That

is so lame," Shaniqua said. "Going with a group of girls screams, 'I'm a loser.' I don't have a date, so I'm going with my girlfriends."

"Well, it looks like you don't really have an option, now do you?" Brittany said. "Jordan ain't thinking about you."

Shaniqua felt the sting of Brittany's dagger in her back. She was certain that the wound was unleashing thick, flaming blood. "Ain't no body thinking bout you. You need to lose some weight."

Brittany rolled her neck, eyes, and head simultaneously. "Oh, believe me they are. My parents will not let me go out with boys while I'm only in tenth grade."

The lunch bell refereed.

Brittany slid her hair behind her ear and clutched her lunch tray with both hands. "I'll see you guys later." Then she purposely sashayed all the way the lunch area to empty her tray, switching her round hips with each step taken, determined to show Shaniqua that she was proud of her physique.

"I think it'll be fun if we all went together. Maybe I can get my brother to drive us," Natasha said. "We'll talk later. I've got to get to class before I'm late. Remember what I said, don't sweat him. All right?"

"All right."

"You still my girl even if you don't get any bigger than a squirrel," Natasha said, hugging her best friend, trying to squeeze a laugh out of her.

Shaniqua smiled weakly and shook her head, while her mind searched and roamed. Homecoming was too big a deal to let her date just slip through her fingers. Everyone was already talking about who was going with whom, what he or she was going to wear, and where everyone would hang out afterwards. Next to Prom, it was the hottest dance of the year. And she was determined not to miss it, but more importantly, she was going to enjoy it with Jordan, not a bunch of loser girlfriends. If Natasha and Brittany wanted to be squares that nobody knew, then they could go right ahead. She was still going to become an 'It' girl this year.

Chapter 8

Shaniqua sat in fifth period Geography,
oblivious to what Mr. Oluwan was saying. She
couldn't care less about Egyptian civilization
or that Kemet was Egypt's original name, or
how the Nile River flows from south to north.
Her mind was focused on more important
matters, matters of the heart. Jordan Kelley.
Homecoming was only eight days away and she
hadn't heard from him since the first letter she
wrote regarding the dance. Her popularity was
riding on this one dance. It would set the tone for
the whole school year. She gave herself
permission to write another letter, but she
promised herself that this would be her last one
if he neglected to respond. Moisture gathered
in the palms of her hands. She slid them down
her jeans and wrote as if she was jotting down
class notes:

Dear Jordan,
What's up? I haven't heard from you in awhile. I

was wondering if we could go to the homecoming dance together. Please let me know ASAP.

Shaniqua

She ripped the sheet of paper in half, folded the letter thinly, and tucked it in her pants pocket until the end of the day. Her thoughts were wild with anticipation. She would be going to the dance with one of the most popular boys in school, and by mere association, she would become popular.

The bell sounded, ending school for the day. She rushed through the crowded hallways to Jordan's locker, hoping she wouldn't catch him there, especially not with Cherise. She turned the corner, relieved that he wasn't there, then worked the note into the crack of his locker door and left.

Shaniqua sat through dinner, eager for the phone to ring, picking over her Granny's delicious Brunswick stew.

Granny watched her from the opposite end of the table. "Chile, what in the world is going on with you? You acting mighty strange these days?"

"Nothing, Granny."

"Don't tell me nothing, you ain't even touched your sweet-water cornbread."

"I'm not that hungry, I ate a lot at lunch."

"Uh-huh," Granny said, giving her a look like she doubted everything her granddaughter said. "Well, you gonna eat tonight, 'cause you already too bony as it is. And don't nothin' want some bones but a dog. Food cost too much for you to be picking over. I wish I had food like this when I was coming up. We be lucky to get some meat. I can remember being happy on Christmas morning if I got an orange and piece of candy."

Shaniqua cleaned her plate to shut her grandmother's mouth. Granny had a way of talking things into the ground until your ears nearly bled. She could easily go from subject to subject without anyone's input. Shaniqua hurried upstairs to her bedroom to do homework, but it was useless; she couldn't focus on anything but Jordan.

By nine o'clock, Shaniqua had given up hope that he was going to call. She figured he probably hadn't returned to his locker at the end of the day to retrieve the note. It wasn't like he was the type that carried books around to class or took home any homework. She laid her clothes out for tomorrow, then curled up in her bed. She was exhausted. Homework would have to wait.

The following morning in homeroom, Shaniqua watched Jordan enter. He was talking and laughing as usual with his buddies, Rick and James. Something shiny reflected light each time Jordan opened his mouth. Mrs. Roberson started with roll call as she usually did. Then announcements came over the PA system when a crumpled up note landed on Shaniqua's desk. She stared at it in disbelief, then gracefully slid it underneath her folder to hide it from Mrs. Roberson. She hoped it wasn't another one of Rick's stupid letters. She thought he had a lot of nerve trying to talk to his friend's girl. Shaniqua wanted to rip the note open immediately, but she needed to maintain some sense of coolness. Her nerves were getting the best of her. She started gnawing on her nubs; the anticipation was killing her slowly.

She could see the vision so clearly in her head. She'd pull her braids back into a stylish updo, allowing a few tresses to dangle frivolously at the sides. Nee Nee would apply her makeup, since she was good with cosmetics. She'd borrow a fancy spaghetti strap dress from her as well, then tell Jordan what color to wear so they'd look more like a couple. They would stroll into the dance and everything except the music would cease. And in one swift turn of heads, she would be made.

Shaniqua clutched the note in her hand as the bell sounded; she would read it on her way to first period. She looked around to see if anyone was watching her. Most of the kids from homeroom had already disappeared down the various corridors. Her shaking fingers steadied themselves as she unfolded the note. Her eyes fell on her own words. It was the same note that she had left in Jordan's locker yesterday. She looked closer. His response was at the very bottom of the paper sloppily written:

Nope, I don't do dances.

An ache swelled thickly in her throat as Rick walked toward her. She leaned against the wall staring at the letter through red-rimmed eyes; her shoulders drooped in disappointment.

Rick grinned. "Hey, Shaniqua, what's up?"

Shaniqua nodded, fighting hard to keep from blinking down tears.

"You going to the dance?"

Shaniqua shrugged her shoulders.

"I'll take you."

Shaniqua blushed. "Really?"

"I gotta go, but holla at me tonight," Rick said, walking away.

Shaniqua started down the hallway, her thoughts were wild. Though her heart longed for Jordan, if she did go with Rick, at least she would have a date and she could possibly make Jordan jealous. Shaniqua turned down the hall and spotted Natasha and Brittany hanging out by Brittany's locker. She wished she could morph into a fly and fly right pass them. Or snap her fingers like Sabrina the Teenage Witch and disappear. She wanted to be alone.

"Over here, Shaniqua," Natasha called down the hallway.

Shaniqua forced a smile. "Hey."

"What's wrong with you?" Brittany asked.

"Nothing."

"It's all in your face, girl," Natasha said, then looked at the note clutched in Shaniqua's hand.

"Jordan's not going to homecoming dance; it

isn't his type of thing," Shaniqua said, hoping she wouldn't break down in front of her friends.

"Are you surprised? The boy barely comes to school as it is. Y'all see his new gold tooth. Ghetto ghetto!" Brittany said, giggling.

Shaniqua slapped her hands against her hips. "Well, at least I have somebody who wants to take me. Anybody ask you?"

Brittany puckered her eyebrows and lips in disbelief. "Who?"

"Rick."

"Rick who?"

"Rick Mathis in my homeroom."

"Jordan's boy?"

"Yep," Shaniqua said proudly.

Brittany scrunched up her face. "Uewww! He's a loser!"

Natasha nodded in agreement with Brittany. "You'll lose cool points big time going with him. Like a minus twenty!" Natasha said, laughing.

Shaniqua thought about it for a minute. Her friends were right. Rick Mathis was a serious nobody. "Well, I didn't say I was going with him, I said he asked me to."

Brittany sneered. "And why do you think fish lips asked you? 'Cause he's hoping you are going to do the nasty with him."

Shaniqua flipped her hand in the air, as if she were flinging off everything and everybody. "I've got to go, I'll see y'all later."

Chapter 9

As Shaniqua dressed for the homecoming dance, she found herself actually getting excited. She decided that it was better to go with girlfriends, than to not go at all. Looking through the half-cracked mirror that hung crookedly on the back of her bedroom door, she had to admit, she looked hot. Her long thin braids cascaded down her back, while her black mini-dress hugged her tightly. She smiled. Though she was petite, she had a nice shape. Ample bosom, a flat stomach, and an apple bottom butt. She stared at herself in the mirror, thinking how right Nee Nee was about clothes making all the difference in the world. She turned to admire her backside. *This dress is slammin'.*

Shaniqua heard the car pull up and the doorbell rung. She took her time coming down the stairs in Nee Nee's three-inch black stilettos.

"Come on in, baby," Granny said.

"Hello, Ms. Williams," Natasha said.

"How you, Tasha?"

"I'm good. How are you?"

"Well, 'spose I'll do for an ol' woman. Your brother's gonna bring Shaniqua home, too?"

"Yes, ma'am."

"All right, y'all look nice. Shaniqua, you keep that dress pulled down, you gone show all yo' business ... you hear?"

"Yes, ma'am."

They stepped out into the brisk night air, the wind clipping their words as they complimented each other on the way to the car. Shaniqua slid in the back seat alongside Brittany, glad to have shelter from the cold. Granny was right she did need a jacket. But hers was definitely too ugly to bring. Brittany passed pleasantries with Nate and then turned to Brittany. "Girl, your parents actually let you come out, oh my God, somebody call Ripley's 'cause I sure don't believe it."

Brittany rolled her eyes at Shaniqua.

Shaniqua laughed. "So what time do you have to be home, nine o'clock?"

"Eleven-thirty," Brittany said, boastfully.

"Dang girl, your parents treat you like your still a baby. The dance ain't even over until eleven-thirty."

"They're just looking out for my best interest," Brittany said in her parents' defense. But deep down, she felt like they still treated her as if she didn't know anything and couldn't think for herself. It irritated her that her parents controlled just about every aspect of her life. She couldn't wear the clothes she wanted, her hair had to be styled a certain way, her mother's way. Her mom would say, "Brittany, if you want to be a professional pianist, then you have to look like one, and not wear some slicked up chicken head hairstyle." Most days, Brittany arrived at school and went immediately into the bathroom to restyle her hair. Then, on her bus ride home, she'd put it back into the same style as when she left home. Somehow, she didn't recall her parents being so strict with her brother, when he was in high school. Now that Kevin was in his first year at Emory, they really didn't have anyone else to focus on.

Natasha, Brittany, and Shaniqua arrived nervously, taking in the scene of their first high school dance. The gymnasium sparkled. Silver and white balloons bobbed around the ceiling and walls, while matching crepe paper swayed in the air from the blowing fans. There was a handsome stage for the royal homecoming court decorated with a blue and white glittery backdrop. The DJ was perched on a platform, playing loud music. The gym was packed with mostly sophomores, juniors, and seniors. More than half the students were coupled up, and the ones that were not, danced in groups.

Shaniqua studied the crowd on the dance floor. "Y'all got me here with y'all, but that's where I'm drawing the line."

Natasha and Brittany gave Shaniqua puzzled looks.

Shaniqua shifted her weight to the other foot and pointed at a group of girls dancing together. "Hell, no, I will not be dancing with y'all. That's just too lame."

"You didn't have to come," Brittany snapped.

"Brittany, shut up," Shaniqua shot back.

"All right guys, can we all just get along and have some fun?" Natasha said.

DJ Monsoon played a crowd-pleasing song, and everyone rushed to the dance floor. Natasha and Brittany followed suit, dancing together. The two had already agreed that they were not going to let not having dates spoil their fun. Shaniqua stood by the punchbowl, sipping a concoction of fruit punch and Sprite, when she noticed two boys huddled together at the far end of the refreshment table. Curiosity propelled her to move closer to see what they were doing. Snooping was a skill she had learned from her grandmother. Granny was forever turning off the lights, creeping around the house to peek out the windows. She'd say "People ain't like they use to be, watching ya house and chil'rens for you if you weren't home. Today, folks barely open they mouth to speak." Shaniqua studied them. Jared and Brandon poured something into their cups from a silver flask. She would have never guessed in a million years that they would be the type to drink alcohol. She had always thought of those two juniors as being square. Jared was a starter on the Varsity basketball team and Brandon was the sixth man. They gulped down what was in their cups and moved from the refreshment table over to the dance floor.

After an hour, the DJ slowed the music. Shaniqua couldn't help looking at the couples dancing together. She wished badly that it could have been her and Jordan Kelley slow dancing. She felt alone at the dance. Natasha and Brittany had found dancing partners, Jared and Brandon. Suddenly, a group of students appeared at the entrance to the gym. From across the room, Shaniqua saw Jordan Kelley's silhouette. She could hardly believe her eyes. Happiness came stealing over her. She smiled, thinking that he had come to surprise her. Her spirits lifted. She fixed her dress, did a quick lipstick check and then flung her braids over her shoulder. She looked up again, hoping to make eye contact when she noticed Cherise standing next to him. His arm was wrapped around her waist. Their outfits were well coordinated in black and white. Shaniqua felt sick, her stomach had plunged down to her feet. Jordan had lied about not coming to the dance. He lied about Cherise. He lied about ever caring for her. She hated him.

She rushed to the dance floor, her arms tucked tightly across one another, creating a forceful stance. "Let's go to the bathroom," Shaniqua said to Brittany.

"You go, we're in the middle of the song," Brittany said, dancing closely to Jared.

Natasha noticed Shaniqua's watery eyes, then looked back at Brandon and Jared. "Hey, we're going to the restroom, we'll catch up with you guys later."

"I'm counting on it," Jared said to Brittany.

Brittany was blushing so hard that her swarthy complexion turned rosy. "Okay," she said, smiling sweetly, letting her dimples do all the charming.

Natasha and Brittany trailed Shaniqua single file into the bathroom like baby ducks.

Brittany toyed with her limp hair in the mirror. "Oh my God, Jared is so fine."

"He is definitely diggin' on you," Natasha said.

Shaniqua stared at both of her friends, annoyed. "He's here!"

"Who?" Brittany and Natasha said in unison.

"Jordan Kelley."

Brittany shifted her weight, slapped both hands on her hips. "And ... your point is?"

"He's here with Cherise," Shaniqua said, fighting back tears.

"Get over it already, damn!" Brittany yelled. "He's just not that into you."

"Brittany, shut the hell up! I'm ready to go home," Shaniqua said.

Natasha saw the raw hurt in Shaniqua's eyes. "Girl, don't let him steal your joy like that. Besides, Nate won't be back until eleven-thirty."

"What?" Brittany shouted. "I have to be home by then."

Natasha looked at them both; she didn't have a solution for either of them. "Brittany, we said eleven-thirty in the car."

"Well, I thought the dance was over at eleven. That's what I told my parents."

Natasha shrugged her shoulders. "Well, he may come back sooner, I don't know."

"Can't you call him?" Brittany asked.

"Yeah, Tasha, try to call him," Shaniqua chimed in.

"No, guys, I can't. He's not my personal chauffeur. When Nate drops me off, he goes and does his thing until it's time to pick me up. He's not going to stop what he's doing to come get me unless it's an emergency. That's my dad's rule."

"Well, I've got to find another ride, I can't risk being late," Brittany said, watching herself talk through the mirror and trying restyle her limp hair. "I'm going to ask Jared. He's got a hot car."

"If I were you, I'd try to find someone else," Shaniqua said.

"Oh, and why is that?" Brittany shot back.

"Because he's drunk!"

"He is not. You're just jealous."

"Brittany, I'm not kidding. I saw him and Brandon pouring alcohol into their cups."

"Shaniqua, I've been dancing with him for the last twenty minutes, so I think I would know if he's drunk. And he's not, so I'm going to ask him," Brittany said, and did a step, turn, pivot out of the restroom as her stringy hair swayed behind.

"Don't leave, girl," Natasha said.

"I can't anyway, I don't have a ride."

"Just ignore Jordan. Don't let him know that it bothers you. Dance with other people. At least try to have a good time. You haven't even danced yet."

"Fine, I'll try."

"That's my girl," Natasha said, patting Shaniqua on the back.

As Shaniqua was going out of the bathroom, Cherise was coming in. The two collided in the doorway.

"Excuse you," Cherise said nastily.

Shaniqua zeroed in on her flared nostrils. "Excuse me."

Cherise bullied her way through the door. "Bitch better watch where she's going next time."

Natasha whispered in Shaniqua's ear, "Keep going, just ignore her." Natasha knew, had they been in elementary school, Shaniqua would have politely escorted her out to the playground and beat the crap out of her, like she did Tiffany Tatum for calling her baldheaded in the fourth grade.

Once they were safely away from the bathroom, Shaniqua cried out, "Oh, no, she didn't! I swear that bulldog-lookin' skank is going to make me hurt her!"

"Jordan is not worth it," Natasha said.

They walked near to where Brittany and Jared were dancing. Shaniqua was fighting mad. "If she says one more thing to me, I'm going to stick her in the jaw! I mean it, Tasha. I'm not playing. Just one more thing."

"Girl, don't let Jordan or Cherise know you're upset. At least try to play it off," Natasha pleaded.

DJ Monsoon started spinning the old 80's rap classics and Brittany and Jared couldn't get off the dance floor. Their bodies were gyrating to the heavy bass, doing the old school dances they had seen their parents do. For a tall, lanky boy, Jared could dance, Brittany thought. Most brothas barely moved on the dance floor. He was definitely a fun partner. Brittany couldn't help but to wonder how she had gotten so lucky. She thought of asking him why didn't he have a date, but then he'd probably ask her the same question. And she didn't have an answer for him or at least, one that she was willing to share. That would be so not cool to tell someone that her parents didn't allow her to date yet. Or worse, no one had asked her.

Jared was definitely feeling the music as if he had grown up in that era. Brittany tugged at his shirt a couple of times while he bent over doing "The Butt."

"Doin' the butt," Jared sang. "Sexy, sexy."

Brittany giggled. He was definitely very lively. She thought he would have been more uptight because he always walked around the school, stiff-lipped and quiet. She had only seen him with one girl and a few other guys from the team.

"It's time," Brittany said, sweeping her sweaty hair out of her face and smiling sweetly.

She grabbed his hand and guided him off the dance floor and over to where her girlfriends were standing.

"It's almost eleven, so I'm about to leave," Brittany said, looking down at her watch and then her freshly manicured hand. "Jared's giving me a ride."

"I'll be back, I'm going to tell my partner," Jared said and walked off.

"Okay," Brittany said, hanging onto his every word. "He is too cute."

"He's cute, but short," Natasha said.

"He is not. He's the same height as you."

"Brittany, that would be five-ten, and that's short for a boy."

"Don't hate, congratulate!" Brittany teased. "If my dad calls your cell phone, don't answer. I don't want him to know that your brother didn't bring me home."

"Humph, if I were you, I wouldn't go with him," Shaniqua said.

Brittany scoffed, "Well, it's obvious you're not me and I ain't you. Sound familiar?"

"Will you two stop it, already? Geez," Natasha said. "Brittany, did you ask Jared if he'd been drinking?"

"No. Like I said, if he'd been drinking, I'd know," Brittany said indignantly.

"Oh really?" Shaniqua said, just as Jared returned.

Brittany's smile stretched across her chubby cheeks. "Bye guys."

Natasha winked. "Be careful, Brittany, call me tomorrow."

Brittany and Jared headed for his car, walking hand in hand. At first, she wasn't sure if he had a personal interest in her or if she was just a fun dance partner. But that tiny gesture sealed the deal. He had grabbed her hand, guided her through the thick crowd, and didn't let go until he opened the car door. Brittany slid in ladylike, sitting down butt first and keeping her knees together, she gently placed both feet inside the car. She was so glad that she had worn her olive green dress; it contrasted nicely against his black leather seats. When he sat down beside her, they locked eyes into an intimate dance of their own. There was an electrifying chemistry between them. Brittany felt the current each time he spoke, smiled, laughed, danced, walked, and breathed. He was handsome, strong cheekbones and deep-set dark eyes with long thick lashes; the kind of lashes that girls sought after in gooey tubes of mascara. His skin looked as though it came from the same cocoa seed as hers.

They talked openly in the car, exchanging information about their families and friends, and where they wanted to go to college. Occasionally, Brittany's mind would wander back to the discussion she had with Shaniqua earlier. She realized that she didn't know Jared very well, but nothing about him seemed intoxicated.

"So, do you always go to the dances stag?" Brittany blurted out of nowhere.

"Well, I do if I don't have a girlfriend."

Curiosity was eating Brittany alive. She couldn't hold back. "Weren't you dating that cheerleader?"

"Oh, Kim, yeah."

"What happened?"

"We broke up last week."

Brittany camouflaged her delight, by turning to look out of the passenger window. *Too bad, so sad.* "I'm sorry to hear that."

"No, it's cool. She was too demanding, anyway."

They say curiosity kills the cat, but I say satisfaction brought it back. Brittany smiled. "How so?"

"She wanted to spend every weekend together. I couldn't hang out with my boys without her getting mad at me. She was just way too serious."

Suddenly, a carload of teenagers in a red Camaro pulled alongside of Jared's yellow Mustang at the stoplight. They revved their engine, signaling to Jared they wanted to race. He returned the nonverbal challenge by revving his own high-performance machine.

"Uh, I don't think you should do this," Brittany said calmly.

"It's okay. I'm just going to race them two blocks, that's it."

"I would really rather you didn't," she said firmly. "It's pointless."

Jared chuckled. "It's a male thing, I wouldn't expect you to understand."

All eyes were fixed on the red traffic light. As the adjacent light changed to yellow, both cars revved their engines one last time before take-off. Their windows were open a crack, allowing the rap music from both cars to rival their motors.

Brittany was getting nervous. "Don't do this, Jared!"

The light turned green. Both cars peeled off with high velocity. The Camaro was out in front by half a car length.

Brittany shook her head, angry. His behavior had spoiled the mood. And as her mom would always say, 'It will be a cold day in hell before and in this case, before she ever went out with him again, she thought. She glanced at the speedometer, already at 60 mph. "Slow down!" Brittany yelled, clutching the door handle.

"Don't worry, I got this. Hold on!" Jared said as he shifted into fifth gear.

The race was in full swing and entering the third block. Brittany noticed something moving in the street. "Watch out!"

Jared slammed on the breaks and swerved to the right in an effort to miss the dog. The car spun out of control and skidded sideways toward a large pole. Brittany screamed, but it was no use. Their car hurled onto the sidewalk, slamming the driver side into the utility pole. There was no sound, only the quiet of the aftermath of a crash and the smell of burnt rubber.

Brittany gasped for air. She felt the rush of a warm fluid oozing down her face. She looked for Jared. He was slumped over her lap. Brittany took one last gasp of air, then everything faded to black.

Chapter 10

At dawn, Sunday, the telephone jolted Natasha out of her sleep. She turned over; the clock read 3:57 in neon red. She buried her head underneath her pillow in an effort to get back to sleep, when she heard a light tap on her door.

"Yes?"

"May I come in?" her dad whispered.

"Yes."

It was dark, but she could see his large frame from the glow of the streetlight outside of her bedroom window. Her heart began to race as he took a seat at the foot of her bed. Her face scrunched in confusion. "What is it, Dad?"

"Princess, I'm afraid there's been an accident."

There was silence.

Natasha's thoughts immediately went to her mom. Her voice fell into a whisper. "Has the cancer returned?"

"No, your mom is fine."

A wave of relief washed over Natasha.

Her mom had been diagnosed with breast cancer several years ago. Luckily, they had caught it in the early stages and removed the lump, but the doctors said that there was a chance that it could return.

"What's wrong then?"

"It's Brittany," he said. "She's been in a car accident."

"Oh, no." Natasha was barely able to respond. "Oh my God, is she okay?"

"That was her dad on the phone. He said she's unconscious."

Her crying muffled her words. "Oh my God, what happened?"

"They don't know. Brittany's dad said the car crashed on the driver side. The boy didn't make it."

"Oh my God! Who Jared?"

"Uh-huh."

Natasha let out an ear-splitting squeal.

Her dad wrapped his arms around her while she sobbed into his thick shoulder. After several minutes had passed and her cry quieted, her dad held her by the shoulders firmly. "Princess, I know you're upset, but I want you to try to get some sleep and when you wake up, I'll take you to the hospital."

Natasha nodded. "I need to call Shaniqua."

"No. Not right now. Getting a phone call at this time of the morning would upset her grandmother. Just wait and call later this morning. Okay, Princess?" he said, kissing her on the forehead.

Natasha tossed and turned for several hours, but sleep would not come. At nine o'clock, she showered, dressed, and was downstairs waiting for her dad.

Natasha strolled through the hospital corridors, listening to her dad greet people as if it was a popularity contest instead of a crisis. The hospital smelled like the house of an old person, stale. Though the hospital tried to camouflage the odor with sturdy disinfectants. Before they entered the room, Natasha drew in a deep breath and looked to her dad for reassurance. She was so thankful for him. He always seemed to handle things coolly.

"Go ahead, you'll be okay. I'll wait out here."

"No, Dad, come with me."

Natasha pushed the door back. Her heart immediately fell when she saw Brittany's frame laying soft and lifeless. The nurse was busy checking the fluids in Brittany's IV.

"Hello, how are y'all doing?" Natasha's dad said shaking Brittany's dad's hand.

Brittany's mom offered a weak smile.

"I'm going to check her bandages," the nurse said.

"Tasha, I'll be waiting in the hallway," her dad said.

Dr. Brown, Brittany's dad, followed Mr. Harris out of the room and continued talking with him, leaving Natasha alone with Brittany and her mom.

The nurse pulled the covers back to check the bandages on Brittany's ribcage. The bandages were still clean and firmly in place. The nurse gave a satisfied nod and covered Brittany up, and left the room.

A quiet haze fell.

Natasha stared at Brittany from the foot of the bed. She was afraid to go closer. "How is she doing?"

Mrs. Brown continued staring out of the window. "I think you can see for yourself."

Natasha wasn't sure how to respond. Mrs. Brown's tone seemed mean, she thought. After a few moments of silence, it was apparent that Mrs. Brown was in no mood to make conversation.

"She's in a coma," Mrs. Brown said.

"A coma? Oh my God, I'm so sorry," Natasha said. "If there's anything I can do, please let me know.

Mrs. Brown nodded

"What happened?" Natasha said.

"You tell me. How did Brittany end up riding home with that boy, when she was supposed to ride with you and your brother?"

Natasha felt awful. No words could explain or offer any kind of comfort. Natasha looked Mrs. Brown in the eye. "I'm really sorry, this is all my fault. Brittany said that she had to be home by eleven-thirty and my brother wasn't coming back to pick us up until then and Brittany didn't want to be late."

Mrs. Brown frowned. "Well, all she had to do was call us. And who is Jared Hill?"

"Somebody we met last night at the dance."

Mrs. Brown shook her head in utter disgust.

Natasha's dad peeked his head into the room. "Natasha."

Natasha turned her attention back to Brittany. "I'm really sorry, Mrs. Brown. May I come back later this week?"

"Sure," Mrs. Brown said dryly.

Natasha was glad to be out of the room. The tension was so thick she could barely breathe. She wished there was some way that she could undo everything.

Monday morning, Natasha strolled through a somber haze to her homeroom. It was evident by the look on some students' faces that they were already aware of the fatal accident. Several girls gathered in small groups, crying and consoling one another.

The morning announcements came on as usual. Principal Anderson asked the student body and faculty alike to observe a moment of silence for Jared Hill and to continue to pray for Brittany Brown's recovery. Some kids were shocked by the announcement, but most everyone already knew about the tragedy. Then Principal Anderson advised everyone that grief counselors would be on hand for support. The mood was solemn all day, while everyone tried to piece together what had happened. The rumors were rampant; everything from Jared drinking to them having oral sex while driving.

Shaniqua waited for Natasha at their usual lunch table. Natasha arrived with red, swollen eyes, evidence from crying all night and all day. Shaniqua recognized that look. She had seen it several years ago when Natasha's parents were going through a divorce. Natasha was in the sixth grade and came to school in tears nearly a whole month after her father left home. It wasn't until Natasha's parents sent the kids to counseling and regular weekend stays with their father that they realized their lives would not change. The only thing that changed was the living arrangements between their parents.

"Hey, Tasha, how you doin'? Shaniqua asked, trying to establish some sense of normalcy.

"All right, I guess. Brittany's not doing well. She's in a coma."

"A coma?" Shaniqua couldn't believe what she was hearing.

"Her dad said she must have hit her head or something during the crash and it caused her to slip into a coma."

"How long?"

"The doctors don't know. They said we'd just have to wait and see."

"Oh, my God. Will there be any brain damage?"

"They don't know right now. It's too early to tell."

"I hope she doesn't end up a vegetable," Shaniqua said.

Natasha looked at Shaniqua funny.

Shaniqua realized that her comment was out of place. "I mean, we'll just have to keep praying for her."

Natasha's eyes glazed over the greasy cheese pizza. Her heart was heavy. So much had happened that she hadn't had time to really process that her friend could possibly never fully recover. People were constantly contacting her to get more information that she didn't have. Some students from Brittany's homeroom wanted to hold a candlelight vigil and wanted her to help plan it.

"Are you going to Jared's funeral?" Natasha asked.

"Probably not, I didn't know him."

"Me either. Nate played on the team with him, so, I'm sure he's going. But, I'm definitely not! Brittany wouldn't be in this situation if it hadn't been for him. Everybody's saying that he was drinking."

Shaniqua nodded her head and continued to listen.

"Brandon's saying it was their first time," Natasha said sarcastically, then rolled her eyes in her head. "I feel like this is all my fault. I should have called Nate and had him pick us up early. I know Brittany's parents hate me."

"No, don't say that," Shaniqua said, picking over her food.

Natasha cupped her hands over her eyes to hold back tears. "You should have seen the way Mrs. Brown looked at me yesterday at the hospital. They entrusted Brittany into my care and I blew it."

"That's not true. Brittany wanted to ride home with him."

"Only because my brother wasn't coming until eleven-thirty; otherwise, she would have never gone with him. I know Brittany."

"You don't know that for sure and you can't blame yourself. Uh, I'll be back."

Natasha removed her hands from her eyes to watch Shaniqua dart around the corner.

Several minutes later, Shaniqua returned to the lunch table looking pale.

"Where'd you go?"

"To the bathroom. I feel a little nauseous today."

Natasha cut a curious glance toward Shaniqua. "You're not pregnant, are you?"

Shaniqua shrugged her shoulders and continued staring at her tray.

Natasha glared at Shaniqua with serious shiny, dark eyes. "You guys did use protection, didn't you?"

Shaniqua lowered her head even further. "No."

Natasha threw her hands over her face again and shook her head. "You're kidding, right?"

"Jordan said we didn't need any and that he'd pull out."

Natasha looked up, her angry, red eyes glared,

"No, you didn't! Shaniqua, what in the hell were you thinking?" Natasha said, shoving her lunch tray across the table. "Do you not realize how much HIV is going around? Getting pregnant isn't the worst thing that could happen to you. You could get AIDS and die!"

Shaniqua continued staring at the lunch tray, refusing to make eye contact.

"If you don't care enough to protect your health, ain't no nig— I mean brotha' gonna do it for you! Hell, if he didn't use protection with you, what makes you think he used it with other people?" Natasha said, shaking her head. "And you're sitting up here wondering if you are pregnant. This could be the end of your life, Shaniqua ... your life! Just like Brittany's fighting for her life because of a stupid accident, you could be fighting for your life, too. That's so stupid ... just plain dumb!"

The lunch bell interrupted.

"You need to get checked out as soon as possible," Natasha said, rising to dump her lunch tray.

Shaniqua sat motionless. She had never seen Natasha react so strongly. Natasha never used profanity. Shaniqua covered her eyes to prevent a downpour of tears. She felt so alone. First Jordan, then Brittany, and now she didn't even have Natasha on her side. This was turning out to be the school year from hell. Could it get any worse?

Chapter 11

The last thing Natasha felt like doing this morning was going on the field trip to the High Museum of Art. Mr. Arnold had been bragging for weeks about seeing the 18th and 19th Century British Drawings and Watercolors exhibition. Natasha gathered near the bus with the other art students, waiting for the headache medicine to take effect. She hoped no one was going to bring up Brittany today. She was getting tired of responding, "No change." She held her head steady, nonchalantly watching her classmates goof off, when she instantly remembered, Mr. Arnold had instructed them to dress business causal for the trip. Maybe she would get lucky and he would send her home for being inappropriately dressed in jeans and sneakers.

"Hey, Natasha," Stephen said.

She offered a weak smile, "Hey."

Stephen dug around in the pockets of his khakis for something to say.

"Listen up, guys," Mr. Arnold said. "We're going to start boarding the bus. Everyone pick a partner."

"What is this, kindergarten?" Stephen joked, looking at Natasha.

She did not respond. Her thoughts were miles away at DeKalb Medical Center with Brittany.

"You want to be partners for the day?" Stephen asked.

Natasha nodded and took a window seat near the front of the bus to prevent excessive bouncing that usually coincided with sitting in the rear. Stephen sat beside her. His fragrance was pleasant, clean smelling. His hair was brushed into waves. He looked nice dressed up; a starch contrast to his regular uniform of a t-shirt, cargo pants and old sneakers. Natasha looked out the window to hide her smile.

"Are you okay, you have enough room?" Stephen asked.

Natasha's knees were cramped, as usual. "I'm fine."

They rode in silence while the rest of the kids chatted noisily, happy to be out of school for the day. Her dad always said that silence wasn't a bad thing. It's was good when two people felt comfortable enough to entertain quiet. Natasha was grateful to Stephen for it today.

When they arrived at the museum on Peachtree Street, Mr. Arnold instructed the students to gather near the exhibit that they came to see so they could have a class discussion and then afterwards, they'd be free to roam the museum with their partners.

Natasha moved as gingerly as possible through the museum, careful not to upset her headache. She stood in the rear, while Stephen made his way to the front of the group. He was listening intently to Mr. Arnold's textbook interpretation of a watercolor portrait. Painting was Stephen's specialty, both oil and water.

Natasha's ears perked up like a dog's when she heard Stephen began to speak. "Mr. Arnold, while color is used to convey expression and emotion, I believe it is the unique brushstroke that the artist used that captured the vividness so well."

Natasha watched Stephen come alive with energy and passion. "For instance, the colors were carefully blended to provide an array of different greens in the foliage, but the artist was extremely careful in removing any traces of a brushstroke."

Mr. Arnold sprinkled approving nods throughout Stephen's discussion. With his glasses resting lopsidedly at the tip of his nose and his smile set deep in the pockets of his cheeks, Mr. Arnold was impressed. He looked like an old, happy hippie from the '60s, all grown up trying to live in middle class suburbia.

Natasha smiled to herself, proud that a young African-American male knew more about this era than his instructor. That was a rare treat. *Daddy would love Stephen for this.* Her dad, a DeKalb County police officer, had always lectured her brothers about the importance of a good education. And how society had set a lot of traps for young black men, like guns, drugs, alcohol, premature fatherhood, and how they could overcome it through positivity and education. Her dad would be proud of Stephen, too.

After the discussion, everyone seemed to have a newfound respect for Stephen. He was no longer the shy, quiet boy in art class who never had much to say to anyone except Natasha. He had spoken when it counted and became an authority. They knew he wasn't just taking this class as an elective, art was who he was.

Natasha started playfully clapping. "I'm impressed."

Stephen blushed. "Don't be, it's just what I love to do, thanks to my dad."

"Oh, your dad draws, too?"

Stephen chuckled. "Not quite." It was funny imagining his dad, a straight-faced retired Marine Corps colonel, drawing. "My dad would say, 'Find what you love to do and you'll never have to work a day in your life.' I guess I'm lucky that I found my calling early. My dad would rather I did something more constructive and concrete, like join the Marines. He's hoping that I'll change my mind by the time I'm ready for college. But I won't, I love it too much."

"That's great. I like art, but I don't think that I love it, well, not like you do."

"What do you love?"

"Basketball. I come from a basketball family. My dad played college basketball for Georgetown, and both my brothers play now."

"So, Nate Harris, the center for the JV squad last year, is your brother?"

"Yep," Natasha said proudly. "You went to the games last year?"

"No, I'm not really a sports person."

"And what about your other brother?"

"Neil plays for Miller Grove Middle. He's in seventh grade. He's a starter, too."

"Cool."

Natasha nodded. "It's cold in here. I should have brought my jacket."

Stephen removed his blazer. "Please, take mine."

Natasha let her lips part easily into a wide smile, momentarily forgetting about her braces. "Thanks, I left mine in my locker."

Stephen made the art museum fun. Natasha appreciated his love of art. He had a unique, very interesting way of seeing art. She enjoyed following his thoughts, happy to be relieved from thinking about Brittany and Shaniqua. For the first time in a few days, her headache was gone.

Stephen moved swiftly across the gallery. "Natasha, look at this."

"You can call me Tasha, that's what all my friends call me."

"Okay, Tasha, this is a lovely portrait by Jean-Marc Nattier from the eighteenth century. This was created from black and white chalk. "I would love to do a portrait of you."

"Me? Why me?"

"You have an incredible face and beautiful eyes. Yes, your eyes," Stephen said, staring, already imagining and creating in his mind.

Natasha blushed. Her insides were warm. She slid her hand over her mouth to conceal her metallic smile.

"What'll you say?" Stephen said excitedly.

Natasha shrugged her shoulders. "I don't know."

"Please," Stephen said with wide puppy-dog eyes.

"Okay, but I'm not promising that I'll be able to sit for very long."

"I'm good, it won't take long. How about Saturday?"

A wave of sadness washed over Natasha. "I can't, I'm going to the hospital on Saturday."

"I'm sorry. How is Brittany doing?"

"No change."

"Sorry. I hope she gets well soon."

Natasha nodded.

"Well, how about Sunday?" Stephen said to lighten the mood.

"Sunday should be fine. I'll have to ask my dad, because I'll be over his house."

They wandered around the museum, going from exhibit to exhibit, experiencing culture. It was nice to have a friend to communicate with who could look at things in a more abstract, artistically critical manner. Stephen had broadened Natasha's once narrow views of artistry. There were so many varied forms to appreciate painting, sculpture, and drawing. So many disciplines, periods, styles, regions and genres. She had learned more from him in one day than she probably would have in a college art appreciation course.

Chapter 12

Shaniqua hurled herself out of the bed Saturday morning and scurried into the bathroom. She turned the water on full blast in the sink to muffle the thud of throw up. She flipped up the cushiony blue toilet seat and quietly heaved over the commode, vomiting bitter, yellowish stuff that she wasn't even aware her body produced. This was the fourth day in a row that she had thrown up. She cleaned herself up and then telephoned Nee Nee.

"Hello."

"Nee, it's me."

"Damn, girl, I just walked in the door. I'm about to go to sleep, what do you want?"

"I think I need a pregnancy test," Shaniqua whispered.

"What'd you say? I can barely hear you."

"I need a pregnancy test," she said a little louder.

"I be damn, I'm tired. Shit, I'll be there in a minute. Where's Granny?"

"Downstairs."

"Where are you going to tell her we're going?"

"I don't know. I'll come up with something."

"Give me a chance to shower and change my clothes and I'll be over."

Shaniqua hung up the phone, feeling anxious. She didn't think she was really pregnant, but she had to definitely eliminate that possibility before she alarmed Granny of her health problem. She walked into the living room where Granny sat in a tattered brown lounge chair reading the Bible as she did every morning. Shaniqua stole a quick peek at the blue-eyed Jesus hanging above the old floor model television set and began fidgeting with her fingers.

Granny peered over the rim of her reading glasses, with a connecting tarnished gold chain dangling at the sides of her face. "Where you off to so early?"

"Morning, Granny, Nee Nee wants me to ride with her some where. She said we'd be back in an hour or so."

"Grab your sweater; it's cool out this morning."

Minutes later, the car horn honked.

"Tell that girl I'm gonna skin her hide if she come up in front of this door blowing again. I ain't gonna tell her no mo'. Chile ain't got the brains of a Betsy bug."

Shaniqua thought of not kissing her grandmother goodbye for fear that she might smell pregnancy. Granny had a nose as keen as a Bloodhound's.

Shaniqua leaned over and touched Granny's soft-as-silk cheek with her own and made a kissing sound, the way the French do. "Bye, Granny," Shaniqua said and dashed out the door.

Nee Nee turned into the parking lot of the drugstore. Shaniqua's heart raced, while she sat frozen, unable to get out of the car.

"What you waiting on girl, Christmas? Hell, I'm sleepy. I need to get back home."

"Can I borrow some money?"

Nee Nee snatched her purse from the back seat, pushed aside her wad of singles with her long, baby-blue fingernail and dug in the side pocket of her purse. "Damn, girl, here."

Shaniqua stepped out of the car with a twenty-dollar bill clenched tightly in her hand. "All right, I'll be right back," Shaniqua said, as the wind clipped her words.

The automatic double doors opened on cue, ushering her inside. The store was brightly lit; the spotlight was on her, prompting all eyes to focus on her. The familiar-looking cashier offered her a sympathetic smile. Everyone in the store knew what she had come for. Even a little Asian girl, who couldn't have been more than four or five, stared her down. Shame hovered around her like stale air. At times, she even thought she heard the word "slut." Shaniqua scurried down the personal hygiene aisle. She stole a quick peek at the sanitary napkins section. Tears threatened. How happy she would be right now to wear the bulky cotton pads. She made her way to the back of the store. She had no idea there were so many different tests; some with the words pregnant and not pregnant, others with stripes, one or two. She grabbed the generic brand, that way she could still have some spending change left over. She opted to pay for it at the pharmacy checkout rather than go up to the front of the store where there would be lines and that vicious blonde checkout clerk waiting to offer some more sympathetic looks. She placed the test on the countertop. The pink bald spot at the top of the pharmacist's head, added an even brighter glare. He offered a weak smile, then grabbed the test.

"Is this it?" he said.

Unable to speak, Shaniqua nodded. *What the hell else could I possibly want at a time like this? My whole freakin life is in that box.*

She felt the pharmacist's cold, black irises scrutinizing her, masked in his wicked disguise of indifference. He had judgmental thoughts written all over his sixty-year-old leathery face. She paid him and dashed out of the drugstore.

The wind rattled the white plastic bag. Shaniqua clutched it tightly to her chest and hopped into the car. "Drive!" she commanded, as though she had stolen merchandise and the law was fast on her heels.

Nee Nee pulled up in front of Granny's house.

"I can't go home now. Let's go over to your house."

"If we go to my house, I'm not bringing you back right away. I'm sleepy"

"Fine, I'll walk, now let's go."

Shaniqua went in the bathroom and locked the door behind her. She sat on the edge of the bathtub contemplating. She stared at all the junk in the bathroom. Her aunt and cousin had more body creams, lotions, and hair accessories than a drugstore. Shaniqua was scared, too scared to know the results and even more scared to not know. Her body had already taken on a life of its own. Her nipples grew increasingly sensitive. Her appetite had changed. And now she was vomiting daily. She had heard other girls talk about the symptoms of pregnancy. She wondered if what she was experiencing was real or imaginary. Granny always said, "Sometimes, you could think things into existence."

She read the directions twice over to make sure she didn't mess up the test. One stripe, you are not pregnant, two stripes in the window, means you are. She ripped the testing instrument out of the foil, pulled off the cap and studied the white sponge tip. She slowly pulled down her pants and panties, and urinated, holding the sponge under her urine for five seconds until the sponge was well soaked for a good reading. She sat the test down on the sink to wait at least three minutes for the results. Her heart was beating like a synchronized drum machine. Time was ticking too slowly. Seconds passed like hours. She was thinking of all the possibilities. She stared at the two windows on the test, thinking the number of pink stripes could change her life forever. Would she become a teenage mother like her mother? So much was riding on stripes. She hated them, and quietly vowed never to wear them again. The stripe in the first window had yet to appear. This was the stripe to show that the test was properly performed. Her hands trembled as she reread the directions. She had indeed taken the test properly. She looked again, but there was no stripe. Time had dissolved into nothingness. She looked again, then a pink stripe appeared, confirming the test was taken properly. Her eyes eased over to the next window. There was more nothingness, no pink stripes anywhere. She bit into her nub of a nail, listening to the thump of the dripping sink faucet. Time was evil. Slowly two pale stripes appeared, sealing her fate.

Shaniqua kept her secret. There was no one she trusted enough to tell. She thought of sharing the news with Nee Nee, but she knew Nee Nee told her mother everything. By being only fifteen years apart, her aunt and cousin acted more like sisters, than mother and daughter. They shared everything from cigarettes to clothes. If Aunt Kathy found out about the pregnancy, she would be sure to tell her own mother, Granny. Shaniqua thought of sharing the news with Natasha, but she didn't want to burden her any more than she already was. Natasha had already been worried sick over Brittany. She decided she would wait until the right time to tell her news to the person it would matter to the most, Jordan.

Several days had passed before Shaniqua finally found the courage to share the news. She sat in class planning how she would tell Jordan. She loathed him, yet a tiny part of her hoped that once he found out she was carrying his child; he would want to be with her. She ripped out a sheet of paper from her notebook.

Jordan,
Please call me tonight; I have something I need to talk to you about. It's urgent!!!
Shaniqua

She folded the note and passed it over as usual.

Shaniqua waited for Jordan's call until precisely eight-thirty, then picked up the phone and dialed his number.

"Hello," a woman answered.

"Hello, may I please speak to Jordan?"

A few seconds later, he was on the phone.

"Jordan, this is Shaniqua. I was waiting for you

to call."

"For what? We ain't got nothin' to talk about."

"Yes, we do."

"What! What we got to talk about?"

Shaniqua drew in a deep breath. "I'm pregnant," she whispered.

"So? Why you telling me?"

"'Cause you're the father."

"You's a damn lie! You better tell some of them other niggas you been wit."

"Jordan, I already told you, you were my first and only."

"Yeah, right."

Tears welled up in Shaniqua's eyes. She was devastated.

"Moms already told me about girls trying to trap me."

"Jordan, I'm not trying to trap you."

"Ain't no way that baby can be mine! We were only together once, and I know I pulled out. So you better check some of them other niggas you been with," Jordan said, then slammed the receiver down.

Shaniqua sat holding the phone. All she could think of was that her friends had been right all along. He was bad news. She felt more alone than she had ever felt. There was no one to turn to. Pregnant. Alone. Fifteen.

Chapter 13

Dark skies loomed Saturday morning as Shaniqua peeled herself out of the bed. The constant kaboom of thunder had kept her awake all night. She wished she hadn't committed herself to going to the hospital today, but two weeks had passed since Brittany slipped into a coma and she had not yet seen her. Shaniqua's body screamed that it wanted just to lie in bed. Pregnancy zapped all of her energy. She wondered how something the size of a pen point could be so physically exhausting. She yawned and stretched the stiffness of sleep away, then sluggishly made her way to the bathroom. Morning sickness was fast on her heels. It was a task to hide it from her grandmother, but she learned how to throw up quietly in the commode.

Dressed comfortably in gray warm-ups and sneakers, Shaniqua waited for Nate and Natasha downstairs. The familiar aroma of freshly brewed coffee infused her nostrils. Coffee had never smelled as disgusting as it did at that moment.

She took a seat at the table where her grandmother was sipping out of her favorite magnolia mug and working a crossword puzzle in the newspaper. "Morning, Granny."

"Good morning, baby, your breakfast is in the oven."

"No, thank you."

Granny gave Shaniqua a curious look.

"I'll just have a slice of toast; I'm waiting for Natasha to pick me up."

"You goin' to see about Brittany?"

Shaniqua bit into the plain, dry toast. "Yes, ma'am."

"It's a crying shame what young folks can do to mess up they lives," Granny said, shaking her head. "I keeps her in my prayers. She was such a beautiful girl, too ... just a crying shame."

"Granny, Brittany didn't do anything wrong."

"Don't tell me she didn't. I know I didn't raise you like that. You got better sense than to let some boy you barely know charm you into riding somewhere with him, especially if he's been drinking alcohol. I know I raised you better than that."

Granny rose from the table and wobbled on her slightly bow legs to the counter to pour another cup of coffee. Watching her grandmother took her back ten years to when she used to beg for a sip and Granny would always say, "No, coffee will make you black." Then one day Granny gave in and she took a swallow and choked on its bitter taste.

"Yes, ma'am," Shaniqua said, thinking how she was going to have to tell her grandmother eventually about her situation. But she had to buy some time and try to figure things out on her own first. Maybe after the hospital, she could ask Nate to drop her at the clinic. She heard the car horn over Granny's mumbling.

"Tell that boy, don't blow that horn out in front of my door no mo'. I'll tell you, something wrong with all these young folks today. I believe it's in the chemicals they puttin' in the food."

"Bye, Granny," Shaniqua said, then grabbed her coat and umbrella and dashed out the door. She was relieved to be getting out the house before Granny started on her soapbox of how children ain't fit for much these days. Shaniqua sometimes wanted to mouth off, "Neither was your daughter, my mother, otherwise maybe you wouldn't have had to raise me." But she only thought it; saying it would have landed her in the hospital probably in worst condition than Brittany.

The rain beat down fast and hard as Shaniqua sprinted to the car. "Hey, guys," she said, hopping in the back seat, breathless.

"What's up?" Nate said.

"Hey, girl, how are you?" Natasha said.

"I'm okay, I guess."

Natasha raised her eyebrows, non-verbal for are you pregnant. Shaniqua flashed a fake smile, pretending not to understand. Then she turned her attention to the windshield and focused on the swish of the blades moving back and forth. Shaniqua had succeeded all week long in avoiding the subject at school; Natasha had been preoccupied with other issues.

When they arrived at the hospital, Brittany's dad was conversing in the hallway outside the room, doctor to doctor using medical terminology.

"Hi, Mr. Brown," Natasha said.

"Hello, girls," Mr. Brown said, then turned his attention back to Brittany's doctor.

Shaniqua could clearly see where Brittany got her looks. Mr. Brown had a pleasant smile that revealed the same deep dimples as Brittany.

They pushed open the heavy wooden door. Mrs. Brown was staring out the window, watching the rain slam against the black pavement of the parking lot.

Natasha stopped at the foot of Brittany's bed. "Hello, Mrs. Brown."

"Hi, Mrs. Brown," Shaniqua added.

"Hello," Mrs. Brown said coolly, barely acknowledging their presence.

Natasha and Shaniqua exchanged quick glances.

"How are you?" Natasha said.

"Fine," Mrs. Brown said, taking a seat in front of the window.

Natasha looked at Brittany, comatose in the bed and then checked the heart monitor. "How is she doing today?"

Mrs. Brown continued gazing out the window. "Same as yesterday."

Shaniqua witnessed their exchange, thinking that perhaps Natasha was right, maybe Mrs. Brown really did hold them responsible for Brittany's misfortune. Shaniqua's eyes traveled up the white blanket and zoomed in on Brittany's head bandage, and then back down to the tubes that were cabled through her veins. Her heart sank into her stomach as she looked at her friend hooked up to IV's and various machines. Brittany's 5'5" 150 pound frame now seemed much lighter and smaller lying so still in the bed. Her once vibrant cocoa-colored skin, now had a greenish undertone. Her skin looked more pallid than a decrepit, ailing man. Shaniqua never thought she would miss hearing Brittany speak, miss her cutting remarks. She longed to bicker with her. Seeing someone on their deathbed had a way of putting all of one's problems in proper perspective. Her own problem didn't seem so big now. Shaniqua gently caressed Brittany's hand and searched for comfort in Natasha's eyes. "I feel so helpless."

"Me too," Natasha said, listening to the steady beep from the heart monitor, her only source of reassurance.

"You girls have done a lot, organizing the candlelight vigil. Thank you." Mr. Brown's said, taking a seat next to his wife.

Shaniqua discreetly studied Mrs. Brown. She was a very attractive forty-something, who dressed conservatively with a stylish bob cropped neatly at the nape of her neck. She sat daintily with her legs crossed at the ankles. Her back was erect and elongated. Shaniqua thought how Brittany was definitely a "Mini Me" after her mom. Except Mrs. Brown was long and lean, physically fit looking. Mother and daughter shared the same air of arrogance. But deep down, Brittany would do anything for anyone. Like the time last year, when Shaniqua had forgotten her essay that was due fifth period, and they used their whole fourth hour lunch, foregoing food, drink, and gossip to complete it in the library.

Natasha grabbed Brittany's free hand. "Brittany, if you can hear me, we miss you. Everyone sends their love from school, even your favorite person, Lucy Looty Booty. Other than that, school is pretty boring."

Mrs. Brown stood up and walked closer to the window. Her arms were tucked tightly across her chest. "Well, Brittany will probably never become a professional pianist now. All that time and money, wasted."

The room fell silent.

"Come on, honey, let's give the girls some time alone," Mr. Brown said.

Natasha squeezed Brittany's hand and motioned to leave. "Oh, that's okay, Mr. Brown, my brother's waiting for us downstairs. He has to go to work, so I can't stay long today."

"Oh, I see. Well, thank you girls for stopping by. Take care," he said.

"Bye, Mrs. Brown," Shaniqua and Natasha both chimed in. Without waiting for a response, they walked out of the hospital room and started down the hallway.

"It doesn't look like they are doing much for her," Shaniqua said.

Natasha's eyebrows curled into a frown. This was one time when she felt like slapping the living daylights out of Shaniqua for being so stupid. "Brittany has a team of specialists, including a neuro-psychologist, physical therapists, and highly-trained nurses, all working to help her to ... come out of her coma."

They continued their walk in silence down the long drab corridor. Shaniqua decided it was best to refrain from asking any more questions about Brittany. Her thoughts reverted to her own predicament. "Do you think your brother would mind dropping me off somewhere?"

"Where?"

Shaniqua paused; she would have to quick lie or face her reality. "Downtown Decatur."

"Downtown Decatur, what's there?"

"Planned Parenthood," Shaniqua said softly.

Chapter 14

Nate pulled up directly in front of the clinic. The clouds cast an even drearier look on the plain brown brick building. Already everything seemed drab, even from the outside. There were no windows, no trees, no plants in the flowerbed, just hardened red Georgia clay.

They got out the car and watched Nate go through the traffic light.

"I sure hope he doesn't tell anyone," Shaniqua said, as if that would hold her back from actually going inside.

"You don't have to worry about Nate. He keeps to himself, he would never tell. Come on, let's go in. Oh, and make sure they do an HIV test," Natasha whispered.

They entered the building; it looked just as drab as the outside. Even the red clay dirt made its way inside.

"How may I help you?" the receptionist asked.

"I'm here to talk to someone," Shaniqua mumbled.

The receptionist placed four worksheets on a clipboard. "Are you pregnant?"

Shaniqua nodded.

"Well, I need you to fill out some paperwork first, and then we'll let you see the doctor, and after that we have a wonderful counselor who will talk with you." She smiled compassionately at Shaniqua.

Shaniqua took the clipboard, and sat down near the back of the room on a hard plastic chair. In a strange sort of way, she was glad to see that she wasn't the only teenager who had gotten herself into trouble. Some girls were there with their parents, some with boyfriends and some were with their girlfriends. Each girl wore the same scared, shameful look on her face. She quickly filled out her paperwork and turned it in.

Shaniqua felt an overwhelming urge to cry. Tears filled up and were only a blink away from cascading down her face. Natasha grabbed her hand and rubbed the top of it, the way her mother always did when she wanted to be supportive.

The nurse opened the door, "S. Williams."

Shaniqua wiped her eyes.

"Are you okay?" Natasha asked.

Shaniqua nodded.

"You want me to come?"

"No, I think I'll be okay."

The nurse grabbed a tissue off the receptionist's desk and handed it to Shaniqua. "If you decide you want her back there, I'll come get her for you."

Shaniqua followed the nurse in the back where

they weighed her, took a urine sample and then confirmed the results. The nurse collected all the necessary information and then put Shaniqua in a small room and closed the door.

There was nothing on the walls to take her mind off her situation, nothing to do but cry and think, and think and cry. She was officially pregnant, six weeks to be exact. How was she going to tell Granny?

Someone tapped on the door, "Hello, my name is Sheila. I'm the counselor," she said taking a seat across from Shaniqua. "How are you doing?"

"Fine," Shaniqua said dryly.

"So, you are six weeks pregnant, is that right?"

Shaniqua nodded. She had nothing inside to force words out of her.

"Where is the father?"

Shaniqua shrugged her shoulders.

"Does he know?"

She nodded.

"What did he say about it?"

Shaniqua hunched her shoulders. Then finally spoke. "Said that it wasn't his?"

"Do you know for sure if it is?"

"Yes ma'am. He's the only person I've ever been with."

"I see. Well, do you know what you want to do?"

Shaniqua hunched again.

"Well, we can't advise you, but I can certainly go over your options with you. Would you like for me to do that?"

Shaniqua hunched her shoulders and continued staring at the patterns in the floor.

Natasha waited patiently. She was feeling the heaviness of both of her friend's lives. Her parents always said that high school wasn't easy, but it was some of the best years of your life and right now, she couldn't see how. These were all horrible things, life-changing things that were happening. Jared was gone. Brittany was in a coma. Shaniqua was pregnant. What else?

A half hour later, Shaniqua emerged with bloodshot eyes, "You ready?"

"Yes."

"Can I use your cell to call Nee Nee for a ride?"

Nee Nee arrived twenty minutes later.

"Let me guess, you either pregnant or just had an abortion," Nee Nee said.

"No, I didn't have an abortion. They don't do that here."

"Well, what are you doing down here?"

"I'm six weeks."

Silence had seized the moment and held it tightly.

"Damn, Shaniqua," Nee Nee finally said. "I figured you weren't since you never mentioned anymore about it."

"Did they test you for a STD?" Natasha asked.

"No, they don't do that there either. She gave me a referral to an OB/Gyn."

"Are you going to go?"

"Yes, Tasha, I'm going to go. Dang!"

"So what are you going to do now that you're pregnant?" Nee Nee asked.

"I don't know. I talked to the counselor."

Nee Nee slid the gearshift into drive. "And?"

"I don't know?"

"Well, what did the counselor say?" Nee Nee asked.

"Nothing really. She just talked about my options. I could have an abortion, give the baby up for adoption or keep the baby."

"You know damn well, Granny won't let you bring a baby in that house. You got a lot of thinking to do."

Shaniqua stared out the car window, wishing both Nee Nee and Natasha would shut the hell up and let her be. How in the hell was she supposed to think if they kept asking her questions? She let them carry on about music and videos the rest of the drive home.

Chapter 15

The hearty aroma of fried turkey sausage and pecan buttermilk pancakes filled the morning air. The smell floated up the stairwell and made its way into Natasha's bedroom. She drew in a deep breath, letting the scent fill her. Then she remembered her brothers. She jumped out of bed, threw on sweats, and leaped down several stairs. In her mom's house, she could linger in bed as long as she pleased and her food would remain untouched, but her dad's motto was, "First come, first served."

"Morning, princess, you almost didn't make it," Natasha's dad said smiling, wearing his navy blue "Dad's the Best Cook" apron that he had received for Father's Day over ten years ago.

Natasha opened the warmer. "Two pancakes? Daddy?"

Her brother, Neil, laughed. "Sleeping beauty should have gotten up earlier."

"Shut up, twerp," Natasha said.

"All right. None of that. Let's keep the morning

peaceful," Mr. Harris scolded.

Natasha cut her eyes at Neil.

"So, what do you guys want to do today?" Mr. Harris queried.

Natasha shrugged her shoulders. "Oh yeah, I almost forgot. A friend wants to come over and do a portrait of me."

"That's nice. A girlfriend from art class?" Mr. Harris asked.

"No. Actually it's a guy from my class."

"Oooh, Natasha has a boyfriend," Neil chimed.

Natasha wanted to knock Neil's lanky tail square onto the hardwood floor. "Shut up, twerp! He's just a friend."

"They all say that," Nate, her older brother, said, winking at Neil.

"All right guys, cool it. Leave your sister alone. If she says he's just a friend, then he's just a friend," Mr. Harris said, rising from the breakfast bar. "Well, fellows, it's just us. So, what do you guys want to do?"

"Shoot hoops," Nate said.

Neil looked at his dad pleadingly, "We could use a new Playstation game."

Mr. Harris placed his plate carefully into the porcelain sink. "We'll see. Neil, you clean the dishes."

"But Dad, I did them last week, it's Tasha's turn."

"All right then, your turn, princess."

Neil poked out his tongue.

When the house cleared, Natasha tidied up the den. Her brothers were always eating food and leaving the dishes behind. They knew better than to try that at their mom's house. She drew back the draperies to give the artist some natural outdoor lighting. She looked at the leaves on the trees. It was inspiring to see the fusion of green, yellow, orange and fiery reds. She wished she could capture nature's momentary magnificence on canvas. Fall was definitely one of the nicest times of the year in Georgia.

The doorbell chimed, sending Natasha into a panic. She ran upstairs to her bedroom. *Oh my God, he's here. Maybe I should wear my navy sweater.* She checked her braces in the mirror one last time, though she had not planned to smile in the portrait. She put on a little mascara and a dab of peach lip-gloss. Loose hairs waved through the mirror. Natasha quickly grabbed the hairspray and sprayed it on to keep her hair in place for the portrait. She would hate if Stephen's finished product showed wild hairs sprouting out. The doorbell chimed again. Natasha checked herself out in the full-length mirror on the back of her door and then hurried downstairs. She had to admit, she did look cute in her canary yellow V-neck sweater and blue jeans. "Hi, Stephen, come on in."

"Wow, you look great," Stephen said, holding an armful of art supplies.

Natasha blushed, while her heart hammered her chest. She wondered if Stephen could hear it. "Thanks."

Stephen waved to his father, a larger, older replica of him, sitting parked in front of Natasha's house. "He'll be back to get me around five o'clock if that's okay with you."

"That's fine," Natasha said, leading Stephen into a spacious room at the back of the house. "We can do it in here."

A wave of embarrassment washed over her. She wished she could take those words back and rearrange them somehow. For teenagers, everything had a sexual undertone.

"Nice home," Stephen said, looking around.

Natasha smiled, relieved that he hadn't caught it. "Thanks. You want something to drink?"

"No, thanks."

Natasha took a seat on the black leather sofa while Stephen unpacked his supplies. He placed his canvas on the stand directly in front of the sofa. He opened a tray of charcoal pencils, all different lead types and sizes, and proceeded to sketch the contours of Natasha's face.

"How do you want me to pose?"

"You're perfect just like that," he smiled.

Natasha scrunched her face. "Like this?"

"Yes, don't move. I like when portraits look relaxed, not posed," Stephen said, sketching her chin. "You've got great bone structure, Tasha. Wow! Have you ever thought about modeling?"

Natasha giggled; the thought of the jolly green giant modeling anything outside of vegetables was funny. "No!"

"Well, you should. I think you'd be terrific."

Natasha continued sitting easily on the sofa with her hands resting in her lap. She watched Stephen work, looking intently at her and then back at the canvas.

Two hours later, Stephen packed up his supplies in his black case.

"Can I see?" Natasha said, rising from the couch.

"Nope. I'm going to finish this at home."

"Just let me see what you have so far?"

"Nope."

"Step---hen?"

"Nope."

"Meanie!"

"I hear my dad's car," Stephen said, grabbing his supplies.

"Bye, Meanie!" Natasha said with a pouty mouth. "See you at school."

As Stephen loaded everything in the car, a weird feeling of sadness washed over Natasha. Stephen was cool to hang around. His funny jokes made it easy for her to take her mind of all the misery that surrounded her.

Chapter 16

Sunlight rays aggravated Shaniqua's sleep. She rolled over and buried her head underneath her lumpy, flat pillow. Monday mornings were always a challenge to get out of bed. She thought of playing sick to stay home, but it never worked. Granny could always tell when she was faking. And this morning, Granny might see that she really did have a condition, pregnancy. She nibbled on a couple of Saltines as the Planned Parenthood counselor suggested to alleviate morning sickness and lingered in bed for another ten minutes. Crackers worked.

She peeled herself out of bed and headed for the bathroom. She sat on the toilet waiting for her urine to flow. It was taking an unusually long time. Finally, she let out a tinkle, but it burned so intensely, she held the rest in. She showered and dressed comfortably in her red and black velour sweat suit and gym shoes. Pregnancy, stilettos and miniskirts no longer worked. She rushed to dial

Nee Nee's number. She knew her cousin would be angry for calling her so early, but this was a medical emergency, she would just have to understand.

"Hello?"

"Hey, Nee, I know it's early but..."

"It's okay, I'm just getting in. What's up?"

"Do you think you can take me to the doctor this afternoon, I think I have a urinary infection. It burns when I pee."

"Oh yeah, that's what it is; I get them all the time. I'll pick you up after school. You tell Granny?"

"No, not yet. But, I've got to go, before I miss my bus."

Shaniqua stepped off the school bus and out of habit scanned the student parking lot. Jordan was cuddling with Cherise on the driver's side of his car. They looked like two cockroaches making out, brownish-black with sneaky, beady eyes and long, skinny, creepy-looking legs. They could at least crawl into the car, she thought.

Throughout the day, she felt strange walking the halls. It seemed like all eyes were on her. She wondered if paranoia was a symptom of pregnancy. As she walked down the long corridor to her seventh period class, she saw Cherise and two of her friends eyeing her up and down. Then one of the girls said, "Slut!"

"You mean, pregnant slut!" Cherise said, laughing and slapping high-fives.

Their words had cut like a machete. Shaniqua was raging, evidenced by her walk— long, hard strides. Only a couple of people knew she was pregnant, and Jordan was one of them. She wondered how he could betray her so easily, the beady-eyed snake. She retreated quietly to the sanctity of her classroom, though not hearing a word her teacher was saying. How could she give a crap about algebra at a time like this when she had to think about real math in terms of dollars and cents, and how she would support herself and her baby or pay for an abortion?

The waiting room at the DeKalb County health clinic was packed. The musty stench of poverty loomed in the air. Little girls and boys with fuzzed cornrows and ponytails played, oblivious to their runny noses and hacking coughs. Nothing ever seemed to stop children from playtime.

Shaniqua had been waiting for two hours. Her nerves were on edge, but she had to get help. There was no way she could go all day again without drinking or eating. To keep from talking to the willing faces that surrounded her, she studied all the medical information plastered on the walls from contraceptives to AIDS to cancer.

Finally, the nurse called her back, took the preliminary tests and then placed her in a room.

Another thirty minutes passed before an Arab doctor walked in. He had a grizzly-looking beard that covered half of his face. Shaniqua could barely see his lips as he spoke. "Ms. Williams? I am Doctor Quzah. What brings you in today?" he said in a thick Jordanian accent.

"I think I have a urinary infection."

"Okay. Let's have a look at your history here," the doctor said scanning the manila folder. "You are pregnant now, is that right?"

"Yes sir. Six weeks."

"And have you ever been tested for STD's?"

"No sir." She wanted to assure him that she never had a need to be tested. She had gotten pregnant the first time she had sex. But it was useless; he didn't seem to care much. He was going through the motions. There was still a full waiting room and it was already approaching five o'clock.

"All right, we will start there."

The nurse motioned for Shaniqua to lean back on the table and then placed her legs in the cold, metal stirrups. She hated laying sprawled eagle on the table; it was so humiliating letting someone inspect her private parts. The clanking of the metal instruments was terrifying. Shaniqua leaned forward to see what the doctor was about to do, but the nurse restrained her. Shaniqua tried to relax by focusing on the tiny holes in the white cardboard ceiling while the doctor poked and prodded.

As soon as the examination was over, the nurse helped Shaniqua up and escorted her to another room where she proceeded to take a host of blood samples. Shaniqua waited nervously. Twenty minutes later, Doctor Quzah returned.

"Well, Ms. Williams, I am afraid you do not have a urinary tract infection, you have a condition known as HSV."

"HSV?"

"Yes, the Herpes Simplex Virus. Are you familiar with that?"

Shaniqua eyes widened. She could not speak; her words were lodged deep in her throat threatening suffocation.

"It is a virus that attacks the immune system. Once you have been infected with the herpes virus, the virus enters the body, travels to the bundle of nerves at the base of the spine, and lies dormant, inactive. Once the virus becomes active, it travels along nerve paths back to the surface of the skin, where it may cause an outbreak. Many patients will develop sores around the genital area and other areas of the body, and some will not. Now, we did not see any visible sores on you. But I am going to write you a prescription and send the nurse back in to go over some specifics and answer any questions you may have. Okay?"

Tears trickled down Shaniqua's face. "Can I pass this on to my baby?"

"Yes, however, there are some measures you can take to prevent it. I will have the nurse discuss it with you."

Shaniqua sat on the hard cot, devastated. She was deep in her own muddled thoughts when the nurse came in to give her a prescription and a pamphlet. She merely thanked the nurse and walked out.

When Shaniqua arrived home, she ran straight to her bedroom, and collapsed down on the bed, crying quietly. She cried for all the things that were wrong. This was becoming more than she could bear. And now she had to wait at least a week before she could find out if she was HIV positive or not. Though the nurse kept reiterating the fact that even if she did not receive a phone call from the clinic in the next couple of weeks stating she was HIV positive, there was always a chance it could show up later, sometimes it could take as long as ten years. This was beginning to feel more and more like a nightmare with each passing day. This was never supposed to happen to her. She cried herself to sleep.

The phone rang, waking Shaniqua from a catnap.

"Hello." Both Granny and Shaniqua answered at the same time.

"Uh, is this Shaniqua's grandmother?" The unrecognizable female voice asked.

Shaniqua heard snickering on the phone.

"Yes, who wants to know?" Granny said.

"Your granddaughter is pregnant," the voice said, then hung up.

Shaniqua thought her grandmother would not have to kill her, because she was going to die right there in her bed.

"Shaniqua?" Granny yelled.

"Ma'am?"

"Come down here right this minute!"

Now it was time for her to die, she thought, as she climbed out of bed. Her heart was pounding in chest as she walked into the kitchen where Granny was sitting calmly at the table. She stopped a few feet away and began fidgeting with her fingers, "Ma'am?"

"Who was that just called the house?"

Shaniqua kept her swollen red eyes fixed on the stained green and white checkered linoleum, "I don't know."

"Girl, don't lie to me!"

"I'm not."

"You sassin' me?"

"No, ma'am."

"They said you pregnant, well, is you?"

A massive ache formed in Shaniqua's throat, silencing her. Shaniqua stood pondering, debating if she should lie to buy herself some time, or come right out with the truth. She toyed nervously with her fingers while tears formed in her eyes. She looked at the patio doors that had moisture trapped between the double-pane windows, preventing her from seeing the tiny concrete slab of a patio. She scanned the heavily fruit-decorated kitchen. The loud wallpaper. The tin sculptured apples and grapes hinged against the wall above the sink. The tattered throw rug underneath the table. The watermelon clock above the doorway.

"Chile, you ain't deaf!" Granny said, getting angry. "If I ask you a question, I 'spect a response. You pregnant?"

"Yes, ma'am."

"For crying out loud. Lawd have mercy! Lawd Lawd Lawd! I just don't know what to say. I declare, Shaniqua, you 'spose to be smarter than that. Now you headed down the same road as yo' momma, having babies too young. But at least yo' momma was sixteen. How old you is?"

"Fifteen."

"Good God almighty. Just a baby having a baby! I declare."

Shaniqua stood quietly leaning up against the kitchen sink. She was surprised Granny was taking it so well. Maybe Granny was going to ask her to leave and that's why she didn't have a need to get worked up.

"How you get yourself in this mess ... I ain't seen no boy come round here?"

"It's a boy from school," Shaniqua said, drying her eyes a bit.

"Does he know?"

"Sort of. He doesn't believe it's his."

"Well, is it?" Granny said.

Granny's skepticism hurt. Why did everyone question her as if she was the town slut? She had only been with one boy, one time, and everyone doubted her. "Yes, Granny, I'm positive. He was the only one."

"Who's that boy's momma?"

Shaniqua shrugged her shoulders. "I have his phone number, though."

"Dial it."

Shaniqua's fingers trembled as she dialed Jordan's phone number. She had hoped he would not answer. She could not trust what he might say and then Granny would have to unleash a can of whip ass on him. She was known in the family for putting folks in their place. Like the time during Christmas dinner, the whole family was gathered around feasting, when Uncle Darryl came in and fixed a plate. Granny told him, 'Touch any of this food and I'll split your head wide open.' And that was for not helping to paint the dining room for Christmas.

"Hello?" a woman answered.

"Shaniqua, what you say that boy's name is?"

"Jordan ... Kelley."

"Hi, uh, Mrs. Kelley, please?"

"This is."

"This is Mrs. Williams, Shaniqua's grandmother."

"Who?"

"My granddaughter is friends with your son."

"I'm sorry, I'm not familiar with her."

"Well, anyway, apparently they are pretty good friends, because my granddaughter is pregnant by him."

"What?" Ms. Kelley shrieked. "That can't be possible."

"Well, it is. Hold on, I'll let Shaniqua tell you herself," Granny said, shoving the phone at her.

Shaniqua grabbed the phone in slow motion. She hadn't wanted to talk to Jordan Kelley's mother. That wasn't her place. Jordan needed to deal with her. "Yes, ma'am?"

"How far along are you?"

"'bout six weeks."

"Are you sure it's Jordan's, because he's been going with Cherise since the summertime."

Damn it! Shaniqua wanted to shout. I'm not a slut! I've only been with one boy, one time! "Yes, ma'am I'm sure."

"Well, what are you going to do?" Ms. Kelley said pointedly.

"I don't know," Shaniqua said quietly.

"... cause we can't afford no babies, hell, I have a hard enough time feeding my own damn kids."

"Yes, ma'am."

"Well, I'll talk to Jordan when he comes home tonight."

"Yes, ma'am."

"All right, bye," Ms. Kelley said.

Shaniqua hung up, but her mind was on their conversation. Why did he lie about having a girlfriend when he's been going out with Cherise for months? She hated him. And now she was beginning to hate herself for ever getting involved.

"If it wasn't for bad news, I swear fo' God, sometimes I wouldn't have no news at all," Granny said, rising from the kitchen table. "I thought you were gone be different, do something with your life. But you trying to walk in yo' momma's footsteps.

Well, I 'spose God don't give us nothing we can't handle," Granny mumbled underneath her breath.

Shaniqua listened, but refrained from speaking. Granny was talking as if she had already made her decision on what she was going to do. Shaniqua knew she was not ready to be someone's mother, she still had goals she wanted to pursue. She had always dreamed of doing hair professionally and planned on going to cosmetology school after graduation. And having a baby did not fit in with that goal. Yet, she knew having an abortion went against her Christian principals. One thing was for certain, she was not going to give up her baby for adoption and make it feel unloved, rejected-- the way she had.

Chapter 17

The next morning, Shaniqua was busy organizing her locker, when she heard someone shout, "There she is!"

She turned around to see Jordan and a crowd of students making their way toward her.

"Bitch, why you tell my momma them damn lies?" Jordan said, moving closer in Shaniqua's face.

Shaniqua looked at all the people surrounding her and then back at Jordan. His voice was hard as iron. His eyes were intense. His nostrils flared like a bull. She had heard that some boys beat on girls, but it had never happened to anyone that she knew. Tears swelled, she searched the crowd for help, but all she saw were faces that were looking for some excitement at her expense. She had only had one fight before and now she had to contend with a raging bull. Perhaps she could win, she thought. She had her own fury to unleash. A part of her wanted to shout, "Why'd you get me pregnant and give me herpes, you asshole!" But she'd be sure to lose the fight. Jordan moved within inches of Shaniqua. She felt his hot demonic breath against her face. Her heart was pounding faster; she needed to use the bathroom, she hoped it would not trickle down her pants legs. She studied his cold, angry eyes. *He never really loved me. He was only using me.*

"Back up off her!" The voice seemed to come out of nowhere. "Back the hell up, I said."Natasha's brother, Nate, pushed through the crowd.

Jordan turned his attention to Nate and flexed his arms, ready to fight. "Or what?"

Nate drew back his tight fist, then landed a hefty haymaker to Jordan's temple knocking him to the floor. The crowded dispersed immediately when they heard the assistant principal coming. "Break it up!" Mr. Canada said, looking down at Jordan and then up at Nate. "What's going on here?"

Nate stood quietly.

"Nathan, I'm not use to this type of behavior from you. You've been here three years and I've never had a problem out of you. And as a basketball player, you should know better." Mr. Canada said, trying to help Jordan to his feet. "What has gotten into you?"

"I can explain," Shaniqua said.

"Well, somebody had better start talking. I want to see all three of you in my office now,"

Mr. Canada said, ushering the students down the hallway.

"Get off of me, man!" Jordan said, flinging himself from Mr. Canada's grip.

"All right, young man, settle down."

"Man, I didn't even do nothin'," Jordan said, in a whiny voice.

"Well, we're going to get to the bottom of this. I will not tolerate this kind of behavior in my school. This is inexcusable. All of you know better and I'm sure your parents can attest."

They walked into the front office.

"Mrs. Gilmore, hold my calls please, I'll be in my office," Mr. Canada said to his secretary, then turned his attention to the students. "Have a seat. Now, who wants to tell me what happened?"

No one spoke.

"Well, don't all speak at once? Jordan, you are in and out of my office more than I am. What's going on here?"

Silence loomed.

"Well, if no one wants to talk, perhaps I'll just suspend all three of you from school."

Shaniqua thought about it for a minute. Granny really would put her six feet under if she was suspended. "Mr. Canada, this is all my fault..."

"You damn skippy!" Jordan shouted.

"What's your name, young lady?"

"Shaniqua Williams."

"What grade are you?"

"Tenth grade, sir."

"All right, Ms. Williams, tell me what happened."

Shaniqua stole a peek at Jordan. She was trying to decide how much information to divulge. She wondered if she should tell that she was pregnant by Jordan and that he had given her herpes. A part of her wanted Mr. Canada to know; perhaps that would make Jordan take some responsibility for his actions. But then again, it would bring even more embarrassment than it already had for her. If she told the whole truth, Jordan would be even angrier with her, but if she didn't, then Nate would be in a lot of trouble on her account. She didn't know what to say. "Jordan and I were having a disagreement and ..."

"What sort of disagreement?" Mr. Canada said, peering over the rim of his glasses, while the light shined squarely on his baldhead.

"Sir, Nate had nothing to do with it."

"Who hit you?" Mr. Canada said, turning to Jordan.

"He did," Jordan said, pointing to Nate. "I didn't even do anything to him."

"You were about to jump on her," Nate said.

"Man, please," Jordan said.

"Is that true, Shaniqua?" Mr. Canada asked. Shaniqua offered a hesitant nod.

"All right, well, you fellows are both suspended for three days. This behavior is intolerable under any circumstances. Ms. Williams, you are free to go. My secretary will write your excuse for class."

"Yes, sir."

Shaniqua left the office feeling terrible for Nate. He was only trying to defend her, and now he was suspended. She had heard that suspensions stayed on your school record. She knew Nate was hoping to get a basketball scholarship to college. She only hoped that this would not ruin his chances, and thus his life.

For the remainder of the day, Shaniqua's thoughts were on Nate. He was the only one who had ever stepped in and stood up for her. It was bad enough that Jordan had shared her personal business, but to challenge her in front of the whole school as though he was going to jump on her was catastrophic. After today's event, everyone would know about her.

Later that evening, Shaniqua telephoned Natasha.

"Hello?" Natasha answered.

"Hey girl, it me," Shaniqua said. "Is everything okay with your brother?"

"He's suspended for three days. But I think my dad is planning to take him to school tomorrow and talk to the principal."

"So, your parents aren't mad at him?"

"No, they said what he did was right. And that Jordan had no business trying to fight you."

"Are your parents mad at me?"

"Girl, no. We did have to tell them you're pregnant, though."

"Geez, the whole world's going to know. This is so embarrassing."

"Have you given any thought to what you are going to do?"

"Day and night, it's all I can think about. Tasha, I'm not ready to be a mother."

"Have you told your grandmother?"

"Oh my God, I didn't get a chance to tell you what happened, because I was in the nurse's office lying down at lunchtime."

"What?"

"Yes, Granny knows. Someone called the house last night. That's why Jordan got all in my face this morning because my grandmother called his mother to tell her."

"Who would do something like that?"

"Probably Cherise, she seems to hate me so much. But I can't worry about that now. Hey, is Nate home? I'd like to thank him?"

"No, he and Neil are at the basketball court getting ready for tryouts. Neil's going out for the middle school team."

"Are you trying out?"

Natasha sighed. "I still don't know."

"Tasha, you better. Brittany would want you to."

"We'll see."

"Okay girl, I'll see you tomorrow."

Chapter 18

For days, Shaniqua and Granny went round
and round about what she should do about the
pregnancy. The more her grandmother disagreed
with her decision, the stronger Shaniqua felt
about her choice. She understood Granny's position,
that it was sinful to have an abortion. And that
God didn't make mistakes. Her grandmother
continually argued that if her mother had thought
like that, then she would not be here today.
Whenever Granny made that argument, a part of
Shaniqua wanted to scream out, "Maybe she should
have aborted me! It would have been just as well.
Look at the kind of mother she is to me. She aborted
me after she birthed me. And I'd rather not be a
mother, than be a sorry ass mother who cannot
provide for my child mentally, emotionally,
physically and financially." She wanted to tell her
grandmother all about the quiet pain that she felt
just beneath the surface of her skin. Though her
grandmother did the best she could to provide for

her, Shaniqua still longed for parental love. Nothing could ever take their place; which is why adoption was not an option for her. Shaniqua believed no matter how much adoptive parents loved their adopted children, the child will always have a void in their life from their biological parents. And when this void becomes overwhelming, their sole mission in life is to search for those parents. Shaniqua contended that she had seen this scenario played out at least a thousand times on the talk shows. And the last thing she wanted was a twenty-something knocking on her door.

The night before the scheduled procedure, Shaniqua agonized over her situation. She tossed and turned for two hours, but sleep would not come. She picked up the phone and dialed.

"Hello?"

"Hello, Mrs. Harris. This is Shaniqua. I'm sorry to call so late, but may I please speak to Natasha?"

"It's okay, dear. How are you feeling?"

"Fine."

"Good. Hold on, I'll get her. She may already be asleep, though."

"Hello," Natasha answered groggily.

"Hey girl, tomorrow's the day," Shaniqua said in a barely audible voice.

"Shaniqua, you don't have to do it."

"Yes, I do."

"No, you don't. Why don't you just have the baby and give it up for adoption?"

"Tasha, I already told you. I don't want to do that. You have a mother and father who love you very much, so you don't know what that void feels like. I do."

"There are a lot of people that would love to have the baby."

"No, Tasha, I don't want to go through with it. I made up my mind. I don't want to have a baby, no matter what. I don't want to keep it and I don't want to give it up. I don't want to have a baby. I can't. Not right now." Shaniqua was crying. The more Shaniqua wiped her eyes, the faster the tears came.

"Don't cry, girl. I understand. I'm here for you."

Shaniqua's voice became childlike. "I'm afraid."

"You want me to come with you?"

"No. Nee Nee's coming. She's had one before. She said 'Ain't nothin' to it. But I'm still scared."

"It's going to be okay. Try to get some rest and call me when you finish tomorrow."

"Okay."

"Cheer up. I love you, girl. Everything's going to be all right."

"Thanks. I love you, too," Shaniqua said, smiling through tears.

She hung up the phone and lay in her bed, listening to the constant hum of the quiet house. Occasionally, the furnace kicked on to break the monotony. She tossed and turned, searching for a comfortable spot. She curled up into a fetal position and before long, anxiety found its way into Shaniqua's subconscious. The room was shifting about, suddenly springing to life. She could only see a blur of the pale hospital room and the even paler doctor. The room was spinning to the point where she could no longer put a face to the harsh voice she heard. "I'm sorry, we weren't able to get it all out. Your baby will have to be born deformed."

Shaniqua screamed out at the top of her lungs. The sound of her own ear-splitting squeal startled her. She felt her body jolt itself violently. Her T-shirt, hair, and body were all drenched with perspiration. She raised her head sluggishly and lowered it again to wipe the fusion of tears and sweat onto her pillow.

When the alarm sounded at 5:30 a.m., Shaniqua hit the snooze button and lingered in the bed a few minutes longer, gathering her thoughts. She needed a moment to talk with God, to beg for forgiveness, to plead for His mercy. She vowed to never to get caught in this situation again, if He would just help her through this one time. She showered and dressed in a loose fitting warm-up suit. As she walked downstairs, she heard noise coming from the kitchen. "Granny?"

"Good morning," Granny said, less cheerful than usual.

"What are you doing up so early?"

"I wanted to talk with you before you left. Are you sure this is what you want to do, baby?"

"Granny, I've been thinking about this long and hard, it's the best thing for me right now."

"Well, just so you know where I stand. God don't give us nothing we can't handle. That which don't break your back, make you stronger."

"Yes, Granny. Well, I feel like I'm already getting stronger. I will never put myself in this situation to have to make this decision again."

"I'll be praying for you. You know Granny don't half trust nothing these doctors say and do, no way."

"Yes, ma'am. I think I hear Nee Nee pulling up." Shaniqua gave Granny a quick kiss and hurried out the door.

She hopped in the car, still scared. Her nerves were raw. She wanted to tell Granny that she was not that confident and she really did not want to go through with it. So many thoughts were running through her mind, but she knew she was not in a position to provide for a baby. She vowed never to be a sorry mother or to dump her responsibilities off on others. She was glad at least one person understood her plight. Nee Nee was not only paying for the procedure, but was also good emotional support. She took the time to explain to her in detail what was to be expected. Nee Nee explained that she could go completely under with anesthesia and never feel a thing. She would never know she had been through the procedure, except for the blood afterwards resembling a menstrual cycle.

Shaniqua made it through and recovered swiftly at home. She stayed in bed for an extra day, hoping and praying to hurry and return life back to normal. Tomorrow had to look brighter than today. This had been the absolute lowest point in her life. Even lower than the time when she was five years old and her mother made a run to the corner store for cigarettes and promised to bring her back a Tootsie roll pop, the purple one, and didn't return until four years later. The words, "Momma be right back," echoed in her mind while she waited that day on the porch in the scorching Georgia sun for hours, playing jacks over and over again, until her fingers were raw from scraping the concrete. Then finally, Granny made her come into the house to get ready for bed.

Tomorrow she would tell Jordan's mom that she had terminated her pregnancy. She wondered if she should tell her about the herpes too. Maybe Jordan really doesn't know he has it. The doctor did say that ninety percent of the people who have it do not actually know they are infected. The pain medication relaxed her while she waited on Granny's Brunswick stew and sweet-water cornbread.

Chapter 19

Two days later, Shaniqua returned to school. It felt good to have her energy back. She even felt like wearing her contacts lenses again. Jordan walked into homeroom, oblivious to everyone except his boys. It was actually a relief that he was not paying her any attention. Since she made the phone call to his mother, things would subside. She had even pushed past personal embarrassment to let Jordan's mom know he was infected. She did the honorable thing, now it was up to him to get checked out. The snickers and sneers in the hallway were constant; Shaniqua kept her head high and ignored them.

She met with Natasha at their usual spot. "Hey girl," Shaniqua said with more enthusiasm than she had displayed in months.

"Hey," Natasha said dryly. "How are you feeling?"

Shaniqua smiled. "Better, much better. It feels good to have energy again." Her smile faded. "I know people are talking about me, though."

"Don't sweat it. If you can make it through that, you can get through anything."

Shaniqua thought about the herpes. She wondered if she should let her best friend know.

An eerie silence fell.

"How's Brittany?" Shaniqua said.

"Same. Nate's taking me to the hospital Saturday morning if you want to come. I wanted to go today after practice, but my mom said I should wait until the weekend."

"Sure, I'll go."

Shaniqua went home feeling a sense of normalcy returning. She greeted Granny in the kitchen and they chatted while she ate a slice of pecan pie that Granny had made especially for her. Enjoying the pie, made Shaniqua recall the time when she was trying to explain Pi to Granny and she said, "The only kind of pie I want to deal with, is the kind made with flour and sugar." Shaniqua would always chuckle at Granny's sense of humor. Like the time when Shaniqua was in eighth grade learning algebra, Granny said, "What you 'spose to do with x? That don't make sense to me, putting letters and numbers in a math problem. As long as I done lived, I ain't never had to go to no store and use no letters for money." Granny always had away of making light of things. She and Granny weaved in and out conversations as easily as they had before. Shaniqua realized how grateful she was to have her grandmother in her life. Even though, their views were very different on some issues, she wouldn't trade Granny for the world.

Later that evening just as Shaniqua was getting ready for bed, the phone rang. She grabbed it on the first ring. "Hello."

"Shaniqua, Brittany's mom just called and said Brittany's trying to come out of her coma," Natasha said, full of excitement.

"Are you serious?"

"Yes, she said that Brittany's slowing coming to. She was awake for a few minutes today."

"This is great news. I can't wait to see her."

Saturday morning, Brittany's hospital room was full to capacity with her family. Balloons, flowers and greeting cards were in stiff competition for space. Everyone seemed to be in good spirits and speaking at normal voice levels instead of the hushed tones that was so typical in hospital rooms. Natasha and Shaniqua finally made their way into the room. They inched toward the bed only to discover it was empty. Shaniqua and Natasha looked at each other nervously. Natasha looked at the heart monitor. It was flat lined.

"Hi, girls," Mrs. Brown said, greeting both of them with hugs. "Everyone, this is Natasha and Shaniqua, Brittany's two schoolmates."

A host of salutes resonated.

Mrs. Brown draped her arm around Natasha's shoulders. "Brittany is having tests run. She should be back shortly."

Fifteen minutes later, two nurses wheeled Brittany back into the room. Natasha and Shaniqua passed knowing looks to one another. They were thinking the same thing. Brittany did not look any different. Perhaps they had overestimated her improving condition. There was one noticeable sign of improvement, her eyes were open. The girls stood by while family members rushed to her bedside, talking to her in low whispers, one after another. Soon it was their chance to spend time with their friend. They each took a bedside and an arm. "Hey, Brittany, it's me, Tasha."

"Hey hey hey, it's your girl, Shaniqua," she said, looking at Brittany's messy hair.

"Everything's good at school. I tried out for the basketball team and made it. I can't wait for you to come to my games," Natasha said, thinking how she really enjoyed Brittany at her games last year. She and Shaniqua were always the loudest ones screaming out, "That's my girl!" and slapping high-fives whenever Natasha scored. Natasha looked down at her hand holding Brittany's. She felt a slight hand squeeze. She waited to see if Brittany would do it again, before she alerted everyone in the room. But she didn't feel anything more. "Hey, girl, we have to go now. Nate's downstairs waiting. But I'll be back in a couple of days. Take care, girl," Natasha said.

"Bye," Shaniqua added, trying to smooth Brittany's hair down.

The girls said their goodbyes to the rest of the family and left.

"Girl, Brittany's brother Kevin is fine. Did you see him?" Shaniqua said.

Natasha looked annoyed. "Yes, I saw him."

"Where does he go to school again?"

"Emory University."

"Uh-huh," Shaniqua said, smiling.

"Shaniqua please, he is too old for you."

"How old is he?"

"Don't know and I don't care."

"Dang, I was just making conversation."

They continued down the long corridor in silence. Shaniqua could sense that Natasha was being overly touchy. She was unsure what to make conversation about, so she decided it was best to keep quiet. She knew Natasha had been under a lot of stress. She wondered if Natasha felt letdown because she had expected more of an improvement in Brittany's condition. They stepped into the elevator to take them down to the first level. Shaniqua admired the Christmas tree in the lobby, decorated with bright red poinsettias. It was amazing how businesses seemed to skip right over Thanksgiving. "Tasha, your brother is so nice to chauffeur you around everywhere."

"You think Nate's doing this because he wants to? Please. He doesn't have a choice. That's the deal my parents made with him to let him drive the car. He has to take Neil and me wherever we need to go. When I get my license next year, then the car will be ours to share."

"That's cool. He's still really nice, though."

They hopped in the car. Shaniqua was thinking how she missed having siblings. Brittany had Kevin. Natasha had Nate and Neil. It would have been nice to have her own brother come to her rescue. She admired Nate. He had such a kind-hearted spirit. He was mostly quiet when they all were in the car, as if he was merely a chauffeur and nothing else. On the other hand, maybe he chose to tune cackling sophomoric girls out when he drove. He never had much input into their conversations, he only said what time to be ready to go. Natasha kept close watch on the time when Nate was involved. And Nate never kept Natasha waiting unnecessarily. It seemed their parents had trained them well.

Shaniqua examined his profile. He was very tall, good-looking, with an athletic build that came from years of playing basketball.

"How's Brittany?" Nate asked.

"Her eyes are open now," Natasha said.

"Are they any other responses?"

"No, just the eyes," Natasha said, choosing not to disclose the hand squeeze she thought she felt earlier. She dismissed it as just a figment of her imagination.

"It's been what, four weeks since the accident?" Nate said.

"Yep," Shaniqua offered.

"I hope she's not entering into the vegetative stage," Nate said.

"No, she not!" Natasha shouted.

Everyone was silenced by the outburst.

"Only after three months will someone be considered in the vegetative stage. I know, I've researched it," Natasha said defensively.

They arrived in front of Shaniqua's house. She said her goodbyes and went inside. It pained her to see Natasha being so optimistic. Brittany's fate still remained uncertain. Now that her situation had been resolved, she could better focus on Brittany. Even though her grandmother always cautioned, "Think about others, and your problems won't seem so bad," she had been unable to do it. Her pregnancy had seemed insurmountable. But Brittany needed her now more than ever. She would pray for her. Maybe Mrs. Brown would allow her to do Brittany's hair on their next visit.

Chapter 20

A week later, Natasha was sitting in French class listening to the teacher conjugate verbs into plural form, when the classroom phone rang. Madame Knight spoke briefly and then hung up. She looked at Natasha sitting toward the back of the room. "Natasha, will you come here, please?" Madame Knight said pulling out a pad of pink hall passes from her desk drawer.

Natasha bit her bottom lip. Whatever Madame Knight wanted was serious. She rarely spoke English during class and never allowed her students to speak it. Natasha was uncertain how to respond. She nodded her head and began walking to the front of the class. Her nerves were at an all time high. She felt her height was steadily increasing by the inch with each step taken. *Ho ho ho, green giant.*

"Take your books; you won't be back in time," Madame Knight added.

Now Natasha was scared. She turned around and walked back to her desk to gather her belongings. She knew the whole class was staring and thinking the same thing, the jolly green giant was in trouble. She slowly stuffed her French book and folder in her backpack. She could not help but wonder where Madame Knight was sending her. She had not done anything wrong. She walked back to the front of the classroom and stood to the side of Madame Knight's desk waiting for her to finish jotting down her homework assignment. "You are wanted down in the office, you have a phone call."

Natasha scrunched her face in confusion. "Oh, okay."

"Here's your homework assignment. We'll see you tomorrow," Madame Knight said, expressionless.

Natasha's heart was pounding hard as she made her way to the office. Her thoughts went immediately to Brittany. She walked up to the receptionist and spoke through red-rimmed eyes. "Hi, I'm Natasha Harris. I was told to come to the office for a phone call."

"Oh, yes, Natasha. You can take it over here," the secretary said.

Natasha went around the counter and used the phone on her desk. "Hello," she said softly.

"Natasha? Hi, this is Mrs. Brown, Brittany's mom."

The sound of Mrs. Brown's voice brought tears cascading down Natasha's thin face. "Hello."

"I called to tell you that Brittany is completely out of her coma and is doing fine."

Natasha let out a loud gasp. "Really?"

"Yes, she'll be coming home in a few days."

"Oh-my-God, that's great."

"Yes, I thought you'd want to know."

"Oh, thank you, Mrs. Brown. Thank you for calling. I'll be sure to tell everyone here."

"Okay, dear. I've got to make a lot of calls, so I'll talk to you later."

Natasha hung up the phone ecstatic. She wiped her tears with the back of her hand, smearing mascara. She couldn't wait to share the news. She'd call her parents, to tell them first, and then waited briefly outside of principal Anderson's office so she could then make an announcement over the PA.

Chapter 21

Three weeks later, Brittany stretched out across her bed doing schoolwork, trying to take her mind off the inevitable meeting. Since she had been out of the coma, her mom had continually urged her to contact Jared's parents, but she was not ready. Deep down, she still felt responsible for his death despite what her parents had said. If only she had taken more action, any kind of action, she thought. Or maybe had she not asked for a ride, Jared would be alive today. A part of her felt bad about being the one that survived.

She could no longer put his parents off; they would be at her door in a matter of minutes. She closed her book and covered her face with her folder.

Mrs. Brown walked in the bedroom and scowled, "Brittany, what are you doing? Why aren't you dressed?"

"I was trying to catch up on my schoolwork. Geez."

"You can do that later. Mr. and Mrs. Hill will be here any moment. Get dressed."

Brittany huffed and then bunched her papers in a red binder.

Her mom started out of the bedroom, then turned around. "What are you wearing?"

"I don't know."

Mrs. Brown walked into Brittany's closet and began thumbing through clothes. The closet was large enough to be another bedroom. Her clothes were organized by colors, her mother's rule. Mrs. Brown went over to the black section and pulled out a polyester dress. "Here, wear this."

"Mom, it's not a funeral."

"These people have lost their only son. They are still grieving and will be for a very long time, and you need to show respect, and most of all compassion, Brittany Ann."

"I don't know what to say to them."

"Brittany, you'll do fine. We are not going to cancel again."

"Mom, I really don't want to face these people."

Mrs. Brown shot Brittany an I-mean-business look. "Get dressed, now."

Brittany waited for her mom to leave the room and dressed quickly in the plain, dull-black dress that she sometimes wore for her recitals. She hated that dress to the degree that she used to love to play the piano. She pulled her hair into a neat chignon and slipped on black sling backs, without hosiery. Her mom had scheduled the meeting twice before, but each time, at the last minute Brittany's nerves would get the best of her and she'd begged her parents to cancel.

Minutes later, a silver S500 pulled into the driveway. It was a newer model than her dad's, she thought, observing them from her upstairs window through the blinds. Her fingers fidgeted nervously. She wondered if they would hate her and wish that it had been their son's life that was spared instead of hers.

Jared's dad was first out of the car. He was tall like Jared, clean-shaven looking. Brittany guessed he was probably the same age as her parents, early to mid-forties. He walked around to the passenger side to open the door for his wife. He used both hands to help her get out. Somehow, they looked odd, like they were not a couple. She was heavyset with a long-flowing wig straddled across her head. Then Jared's dad opened the backdoor. A little girl stepped out in patent-leather shoes, wearing a maroon velvet dress.

"Brittany?" her mom shouted up the stairs. "They're here."

Brittany trotted downstairs. "I know, Mom, I saw them from the window."

"Well, why didn't you come downstairs?" Mrs. Brown said, opening the front door.

Brittany ducked into the kitchen.

"Hello, Mr. Hill, Mrs. Hill. And who is this lovely little lady?" Mrs. Brown said, stooping over to the girl. "Hello, I haven't met you. What's your name?"

The little girl swayed from side to side, toying with the hem of her dress. "Jada."

Mrs. Brown touched her soft, thick ponytail. "Jada, what a pretty name for a pretty little girl." Mrs. Brown stood up, turning her attention back to the adults. "I'm sorry, do come in and have a seat. May I take your coats?"

Brittany swallowed the remains of a chocolate chip cookie, then licked the melted chocolate from her sweaty palm. Her mother would have died had she witnessed that, she thought. *All right, let's get it over with.*

Brittany eased into the living room, trying to not to draw attention to herself. Everyone looked.

"Hello," Brittany said.

Mr. Hill stood up and extended his hand. "Hello, Brittany."

A welcoming smile spread across Mrs. Hill's chubby cheeks. She was a pleasant looking woman with an infectious smile. Everything about her seemed, genuine, except the wig. Her deep-set eyes were sincere. "Hello, Ms. Brittany, it's nice to finally meet you."

Brittany smiled timidly. "Hello, Mrs. Hill."

"How are you feeling?" Mrs. Hill asked.

"Good. Oh, and thank you for the flowers."

"Oh baby, you're welcome. You look great," Mrs. Hill said.

"Thank you."

Silence fell.

Brittany looked at her mother for help.

"I'm sorry my husband couldn't be here today, he

had a surgery scheduled. How about I leave you all to talk?" Mrs. Brown said.

"That's not necessary," Mr. Hill said.

Mrs. Brown nodded as if saying, "It's okay." Then she turned to the little girl. "Hey Jada, I've got cookies in the kitchen?"

Jada's face lit up.

"But ask your mom first," Mrs. Brown said.

"Mom, may I?"

"Yes, Jada, but only two, no more."

Brittany sat in the white high wing chair wondering how her mother could leave her alone with total strangers who had lost their son because of her. Her fingers tried to console her by toying with one another.

Mr. Hill cleared his throat. "Brittany, I know this maybe be hard for you and you don't have to do this unless you want to, but it would mean a great deal to both of us," he said gesturing to his wife. "Can you tell us what happened that night?"

Brittany stalled momentarily, as if she was having difficulty remembering. She had played that scene out in her head a least a hundred times so far. But she was unsure what to tell his parents. She looked into their faces; Mr. Hill sat expressionless, while his wife's smile had morphed into sadness.

"Jared was bringing me home when some other teenagers pulled up alongside of us. The other driver challenged Jared to a race. So, we were racing down the street, then a dog walked out into the street and Jared tried to avoid hitting him. I don't remember anything after that. I'm sorry," Brittany said with tears in her eyes.

Mrs. Hill started sniffling. Mr. Hill grabbed her hand and rubbed it. "Were you guys drinking in the car?" he asked.

Brittany shook her head and then grabbed the tissue that Mrs. Hill was offering. She wiped her eyes, and then gently pressed the tissue against her eyes to help stop the flow. Talking with his parents made Jared's death real to her. "I tried to tell him not to race," Brittany said defensively, crying.

Mrs. Hill got up from the couch, came over to where Brittany was sitting, and wrapped her arms around her. "It's okay, baby. We're not mad at you. It wasn't your fault."

"We knew about Jared and racing. We had talked to him several times about speeding down the street to the house," Mr. Hill said.

Mrs. Hill was rubbing Brittany's back. "And we also know about the alcohol he was drinking at the dance. His best friend, Brandon, told us. Brittany, we'd like to apologize to you. We are sorry for what has happened to you."

Mrs. Hill picked her purse off the floor and dug around in it, searching. "We brought you something that we think Jared would want you to have." She placed a yellow gold class ring in Brittany's palm.

"Mrs. Hill, I can't take this."

"Yes, you can. I know Jared would want you to have it."

"I can't."

Mrs. Hill gently secured Brittany's fingers around the ring and then hugged Brittany tightly.

Mr. Hill stood up. "All right, we are going to go now. But if you need anything, you can call us."

"Yes, even if you just want to talk, call us, Brittany. Okay?" Mrs. Hill said.

Brittany smiled and nodded. A wave of relief washed away the guilt Brittany was feeling. Jared's parents were genuine in their caring and compassion for what she had gone through. Brittany walked them into the foyer just as Mrs. Brown came out of the kitchen with Jada.

Mrs. Hill looked at Jada. "You ready?"

"No, mommy. Can I stay?"

They all laughed.

"Some other time, Jada. Thank you all for having us. Sorry to have taken up so much of your time," Mr. Hill said.

Mrs. Brown handed them their coats. "It's no problem. We enjoyed having you."

They hugged goodbye and left.

Mrs. Brown closed the door behind them and turned to her daughter. "Well, how do you feel?"

"Better, much better. They are really sweet people."

"See, I told you it wouldn't be so bad."

"I know, mom, you're always right."

Mrs. Brown cupped her hand behind her ear and smirked. "Huh, what'd you say? I'm sorry, I didn't hear you. Did you say I'm always right?"

They laughed and headed into the kitchen. Brittany took a seat at the kitchen table. "I want to go to school now."

"Not yet, Brittany, we have to continue with your rehab therapy first," Mrs. Brown said. "You can go back after the winter break. But if you feel like getting around, why don't you go practice?"

Brittany frowned. She thought of telling her mother how she really felt about playing the piano. After being so close to death, she realized that she had only one life to live—hers. She contemplated for a few seconds, then gently seized the opportunity. "Mom?"

"Yes?" Mrs. Brown said, unloading the dishwasher.

Brittany hesitated for a moment. Her nerves had silenced her.

Mrs. Brown turned around to face her daughter sitting at the kitchen table. "What is it, dear?"

"Mom, I don't want to play the piano."

"Wh- what?" Mrs. Brown said. She put the black square plate down and took a seat at the table. "What do you mean? Brittany, we've invested a lot of time and money into you becoming a professional pianist. My god, you've been playing since you were three years old."

"That's my point. I don't want to play anymore. I mean, I like playing the piano, but I don't love it."

"Yes you do, Brittany. That accident has you all messed up."

"No, Mom, I don't love it anymore. You do. Not

me. I'm not saying I will never play, I just don't want to make it my career."

A long, uncomfortable silence lingered. Brittany witnessed the raw pain in her mother's eyes. She knew her mother had always wanted to be a pianist, but her parents didn't have the money for lessons. Mrs. Brown clasped her hands in her lap. She kept her head bent low, studying the wood grains in the table, processing the dissolve of her dream. "Fine, I will call your piano teacher in the morning to tell her we will no longer need her services."

"Mom, I'm sorry."

Her mother kept her eyes in her lap. "There's nothing to be sorry for," she snapped.

A stream of tears flowed down Brittany cheeks, dropping onto her dress. "I'm sorry about the accident. I'm sorry about Jared. I'm just sorry for everything that has happened."

Her mother stared up at the ceiling. Then she looked at Brittany with tears cascading down her face. "It's okay, baby," Mrs. Brown said, walking over to Brittany. She wrapped her arms around her and gently rocked her. "Everything's going to be just fine."

They held each other tightly, though Brittany's mind continued to roam. She contemplated if she should leave well enough alone. "Mom?"

"Yes, dear?"

"Since I'm no longer taking piano, can I wear my hair how I want to?"

Her mom pulled away and laughed. "Oh, Brittany. I thought it was something serious."

"It's serious to me. Can I? Please?"

She nodded. "I suppose ... well, within reason," she said, curling up an eyebrow.

"Okay, how about dating in the tenth grade?"

"All right, Brittany Ann, don't push it."

Brittany smiled. One thing at a time.

Chapter 22

It was Christmas morning, and a light dusting of snow covered the bare trees. Natasha admired the scenery from the dinning room window, while she set the table for the family dinner. It was a rare treat to have a white Christmas in Georgia.

"Tasha, darling, the phone's for you," Ms. Harris called from the kitchen.

Natasha walked into the den to grab the phone; she wondered who would be calling her. She had already spoken with Brittany and Shaniqua earlier that morning. Natasha took a seat on the sofa. "Merry Christmas," she sang.

"Merry Christmas, Tasha."

Natasha scrunched her face in astonishment, "Stephen?"

"Yes, how are you?"

Natasha could feel moisture gathering in her palms. "I'm good. This is a surprise."

"What's up?" he asked.

"Nothing, I mean getting ready for dinner."

"Are you going to be home later?"

"Yes, my family's coming over."

"If it's okay with you, I'd like to stop by this evening."

"Oh, well, sure, let me ask my mom if it's okay."

Natasha put the phone down and ran into the kitchen. "Mom, Stephen wants to come over this evening after dinner," Natasha said, panicky.

"Stephen from art class?"

Natasha rolled her eyes. "Yes, Mom. What other Stephen is there?"

Natasha's mom spun around to look at her daughter. Ms. Harris brows gathered, creating a deep furrow. "Natasha Elaine Harris, who do you think you're talking to in that tone of voice?"

"I'm sorry, Mom. I'm just nervous. So can he, Mom, please?"

"Yes, Tasha, I don't mind."

Natasha scurried back into the living room and grabbed the phone. "My mom said okay."

"Great. I'll see you about six o'clock."

Natasha charged upstairs to change into her new outfit. She originally planned to save it for her interview with the modeling agency in a couple of weeks, but this was a special enough occasion, she thought. She slipped on a black skirt with her new cropped jean jacket and low-heel black boots. She pranced in the mirror. Oh yeah, this is tight. Her lips parted into a wide smile, revealing her metal braces. She smiled even harder–she only had three more days and they were coming off. She had a lot to be happy about this Christmas. Her best friend was finally out of the hospital and recuperating. Shaniqua was finally over her ordeal with Jordan. Things were going well, Natasha thought and would be back to normal very soon.

Natasha enjoyed Christmas dinner with her mother's side of the family. She and her brothers had spent Thanksgiving with their dad. Each year, they alternated–if they celebrated Thanksgiving with one parent, then Christmas would be spent with the other parent. It was an arrangement that had worked for the past few years. Wherever they celebrated the holidays, they were always the cleanup crew. Natasha cleared the dishes from the dining room table and put up the remaining food. Her mother didn't trust Neil to handle her good china. Neil had the floor and trash detail, while Nate was responsible for emptying the dishwasher and reloading. Once the dinning table was cleared, their aunts and uncles would begin the holiday ritual of playing Pokeno into the early morning.

Natasha sat around watching and waiting, occasionally checking her reflection in the mirror in the foyer. At six o'clock sharp, the doorbell rang. The Perrys were the most prompt people she had known. Mr. Perry always picked Stephen up and dropped him off precisely at the stated time. She supposed it was due to all the regimented time he had spent in the military.

"I got it," Natasha yelled, to keep her nosey brothers from heckling Stephen. They had already said they were going to give him a hard time. Natasha opened the front door gracefully, to keep the Christmas wreath from flopping in Stephen's face, "Hi."

"Hi," he said, and then turned back to wave goodbye to his parents. "They'll be back in a couple of hours or so, they're going to visit my aunt in Stone Mountain."

"Come on in. My relatives are still here, so excuse all the noise. They're in the kitchen playing Pokeno," Natasha said, gazing at the big red bow wrapped around a canvas covered in brown paper bags.

"Pokeno? I never heard of it?"

"It's a card slash board game where you can win money. Sort of like Bingo, except you can win money four different ways, Center, Three in a row, Four corners and Pokeno."

Stephen nodded "Sounds interesting."

"It is. Nobody ever wins a lot of money, but my folks will stay up all night playing. Sometimes, they're so loud, I can't get to sleep," Natasha chuckled. "May I take your coat?"

"Oh yeah, and this is for you," Stephen said nervously. It's kind of heavy. Where can I set it?"

Natasha smiled. She already knew what it was, there no way to camouflage a canvas. Stephen had stopped talking about the portrait over the last few weeks, so she assumed that he had found a more interesting subject. Natasha hung his black pea coat in the closet. "Let's go into the den."

Next to Natasha's bedroom, the den was her favorite room in the house. She had so many fond memories of playing board games with her family. Everyone would sprawl out on the beige Berber carpet, playing Monopoly, Sorry, and Life. But the family's all-time favorite game was Scrabble. Many nights were spent challenging and debating words like "wharp" and "IQ." And her dad would always help the kids make a word. She missed those days of the whole family being together.

As they walked in, a photo of Natasha, smiling with a missing front tooth greeted them.

Stephen grinned. "Ah, look at lil miss snag-a-tooth!"

Natasha wished she could have hid the photo beforehand, but her mother said, that no one was allowed to touch her pictures.

The den was a warm cozy room. A multitude of photos decorated the bronze faux finish on the walls. A brown leather sectional took up most of the room, leaving an open space where her brothers were sitting in front of the television.

"Stephen, these are my two brothers, Nate and Neil."

Nate paused the Playstation game, then stood up and offered a firm handshake. "Hey, man, how you doing?"

"Good. You played on the JV squad last year?"

"Yep. You play?"

"Naw, man."

Natasha interrupted. "And this is Neil."

"What's up?" Neil said coolly, still sitting on the floor.

Stephen reached to shake Neil's hand. "I heard you play pretty good, too."

Neil nodded, then quickly turned his attention back to Playstation.

Natasha was surprised at Neil's curt behavior. Neil had teased that he was going to drill Stephen with tons of questions, but then he didn't open his mouth. She turned around, and caught a glimpse of the presents underneath the tree. She felt bad that she didn't have a present to give Stephen. "Let's go in the living room."

Usually the living room, or the "cream room" as they called it, was off limits to children, but she was sure her mom would understand her not wanting to entertain in front of her brothers. And there was no way they were willing to leave Playstation just for her. Natasha took a seat on the cream-colored Victorian sofa. Stephen sat the large canvas down, leaning it against the marble top coffee table, then took a seat at the other end of the sofa. "Well, you want to open it?" Stephen asked.

"Sure," Natasha said, walking around to the canvas. She carefully untied the bright red bow, then removed the brown paper bags that were meticulously wrapped around the canvas. When the last bag was removed, she turned the canvas around. She couldn't believe her eyes.

She cupped her hands over her mouth.

"Merry Christmas, Natasha."

"Oh my God, Stephen. You did this?"

Stephen nodded, but Natasha couldn't take her eyes off the portrait. She had no idea it was going to be a luxurious oil painting. She had been expecting a pencil-sketched portrait. Tears threatened. She looked beautiful in the portrait. It was amazing how wonderful the colors came together. Stephen had blended the different shades of browns together; her face in the portrait matched her skin tone perfectly. The rich yellows in her sweater cast an effervescent glow on her skin. Her lips were precise. Her eyes held the perfect almond shape and were in exact spatial relationship to her brows. "I'm sorry, Stephen, I'm blown away. I don't know what to say."

"You like it?"

"Are you kidding? I love it. It's the most beautiful thing. I'm not saying that because it's me either," Natasha chuckled. "You are awesome. I don't know what to say."

"I was worried that you weren't going to like it."

"Stephen, I absolutely love it."

Natasha wanted to hug him to say thank you, but she wasn't sure if it was appropriate. "Thanks, Stephen. I will treasure it always. I'm sorry I don't have a gift."

"That's okay."

Natasha propped the canvas back against the

coffee table and took her seat at the opposite end of the couch. An awkward silenced loomed in the air.

Stephen glanced around at the family photos on the end tables. "Nice pictures."

"Thanks. As you can see, my mother loves photos," Natasha said, wondering if she should share the news with him or wait until after the interview. The only other person that knew was her mom. "Guess what?"

"What?"

"I took your advice and I mailed in some snapshots to Genesis."

Stephen looked puzzled. "Genesis?"

"It's a modeling agency."

"Really?"

"They said they wanted to see me in person."

"That's great, Tasha. See I told you. You are extremely photogenic."

Natasha blushed. She had heard people say she was photogenic before, but she never thought much of it.

"So, when do you go?"

"In two weeks."

"I know they're going to hire you, sign you up, or whatever it is they do when they like you."

"And I get my braces off in three days. I can't wait."

"Good for you."

"But I still have to wear a stupid retainer."

Just then, Natasha's mom came in. "You must be Stephen."

He quickly rose to his feet and extended his hand. "Yes, ma'am."

Ms. Harris wrapped her arms around his shoulders. "We give hugs around here, baby. Merry Christmas. He's cute, Tasha."

Natasha wanted to die a quick, hard death right there on the spot. She was certain her mother had just guzzled an intoxicating mix of eggnog and brandy.

Stephen struggled to keep from blushing. "Thank you. Merry Christmas to you."

"Mom, look what Stephen did," Natasha said walking around to the portrait.

"Oh, my." Ms. Harris said examining the portrait. "You really did this, Stephen?"

"Yes, ma'am."

"This is quite remarkable. What a beautiful portrait. Stephen, you are a very talented young man."

"Thank you, ma'am."

Ms. Harris glanced around the room. "I know exactly where we'll put it, right on this wall by itself. How lovely."

Natasha and Stephen exchanged glances.

"All right, I'll let you two get back."

Natasha felt a little embarrassed by her mother's last comment. She spoke as if they were dating or something. You two.

"I guess I don't have much choice in where the portrait hangs, do I?" Natasha said, chuckling.

Natasha and Stephen sipped punch and

exchanged funny stories of Christmases past until the doorbell rang.

Stephen stood up. "I guess that's my pops."

"Let me get your coat."

Natasha retrieved Stephen's coat and then opened the door. "Hello, Mr. Perry."

"Merry Christmas, you must be Natasha."

"Yes, sir."

"Stephen talks about you quite a bit."

Stephen looked down at his shoes as if he was searching for something.

"You like the portrait?" Mr. Perry said.

"Yes, sir. It's beautiful."

"Well, he worked on it diligently, day and night. I'd have to tell him 'Boy, get your school work done first.'" Mr. Perry chuckled. "It's nice to have met you."

"Thank you," Natasha said, watching his dad walk back to the car. Then she waved to his mother sitting inside the car. "Your dad seems really sweet."

Stephen's face was beet red. He was speechless.

Natasha hid her smile. "Thanks again, Stephen," Natasha said, and then wrapped her arms around him for a friendly hug. "Next time you're here, your painting will be hanging right here."

Stephen smiled and hugged her back.

Chapter 23

Principal Anderson made an announcement on the morning PA wishing the entire student body a happy and prosperous New Year and encouraged students to get the year off to a good start. Then she personally welcomed Brittany back. All morning, Brittany received hugs and kind words from students and teachers. She was ashamed to admit it, but she loved this attention. It made her feel special.

In her two-month hiatus from school, she had found out about Shaniqua's ordeal and wanted to share the news with her own mother. It was nice when her mom would sometimes act like an older sister, but this was too socially detrimental to risk her father finding out. He'd look at her with a raised eyebrow, and say, "Birds of a feather flock together," and then she'd never be able to go anywhere again and would probably get banned from hanging out with Shaniqua.

Brittany made her way through the noisy lunchroom to meet her girls at their usual table. Natasha and Shaniqua had already begun eating.

"What's up Brittany!" Someone shouted from across the lunchroom.

Brittany spun around, her dimples danced as she waved hello. "Hey, guys," Brittany said, placing her lunch bag next to Shaniqua. She could tell that Shaniqua's experience had changed her, though she wasn't quite sure in what way. She still wore her cat eyes and dressed in clothes that Brittany would not be caught dead in.

"What's up, girlfriend," Shaniqua said, chomping down on potato chips. "So, how's your first day back?"

"I'm loving it! Everyone's being so nice to me, even ol' crazy Lucy Looty Booty, with her evil-for-no-good-reason-self had the nerve to give me a hug. Can you believe that?"

Natasha laughed. "Not really."

Brittany stared at Natasha. Something about her was different, too. "What you so fixed up for?"

"No reason," Natasha said, fighting back a big, cheesy grin, ecstatic to finally have her braces off after two years.

Shaniqua laughed, then suddenly got quiet. Her head hung low, her eyes glazed over her food on the tray. "Brittany?"

"What?" Brittany said, studying the pizza on Shaniqua's tray. She finally gave in to her mom's suggestion of taking her lunch to school; that way she would be sure it was nutritious. She hated to admit it, but she was glad that she had lost weight, even if it took her getting sick to do it.

"I need to apologize to you," Shaniqua said with tears in her eyes. "I'm sorry I didn't listen to you about Jordan."

"It's okay, girl," Brittany said, munching on a baby carrot.

"No, it's not." Had I listened to you and Natasha, I would have never gone through all the stuff that I did. I never told you guys this, either of you, but Jordan ... gave me herpes."

Brittany's hand cupped her mouth. "Oh my God! Did you just say Jordan gave you Herpes?"

Shaniqua nodded her head slow and methodically.

"Are you okay?" Natasha asked.

"Yeah, for now. But the doctor said I'll have to deal with this for the rest of my life. He gave me a prescription to take."

Brittany scrunched her face, "Every day?"

Shaniqua shook her head. "Only when I'm having an outbreak."

Brittany choked back her tears. "I'm sorry, too. I should have listened to you and never gotten in that car with Jared. Maybe Jared would still be alive today." The tears trickled down her face.

"It's okay, girl, it's not your fault," Shaniqua said, reaching over to hug Brittany.

"Friends?" Brittany asked.

"Until the end," Shaniqua said.

Brittany smiled. "From here on out, we'll listen to each other ..."

"And take each other's advice," Shaniqua said, finishing her sentence.

Natasha came from around the table. "All right, all right, group hug."

All three friends hugged to solidify a friendship built on newfound trust and celebrating one another's differences.

"Well, I've got some good news that I have been dying to share with y'all," Natasha said.

"What?" Shaniqua and Brittany said in unison.

"You all are looking at a model."

Shaniqua scanned the lunchroom. "Who?"

Natasha stood up straight, cocked her head to the side in a chic pose, letting her hair brush her shoulders. "Me!"

"Girl, stop lying," Brittany said. "Natasha, you are just a few inches shy of being a tomboy. I can't even see it."

"I'm not kidding. I interviewed with a modeling agency and they want to sign me up. They said that I could be a high-fashion runway model because of my height. So I'm starting modeling classes to learn how to walk and pose for pictures."

"Really?" Brittany said.

Natasha nodded, enthusiastically.

Shaniqua let out a loud shriek and hugged Natasha again. "I'm so happy for you. Congratulations! Now, girl, you are going to have to let me hook your wig up for your photo shoots."

"They are going to teach me how to do my hair and makeup."

"Well, you definitely need that class," Brittany teased.

"Whatever, Brittany. You think you cute just because you got a new hairstyle," Natasha teased back.

Brittany flung her hair. "Long layers, you like?"

"Yeah, they frame your face nicely," Natasha said.

Shaniqua stood smiling at Natasha like a proud parent. "A model? Go on, Ms. Thang. We'll be able to say, we knew you when ... So, what's up with Stephen?"

Natasha blushed. "Nothing. We're just friends."

Brittany shook her head. "Tasha, please, nobody creates a huge oil painting of someone just because."

"Okay, maybe he does like me. I don't know for sure. But for now, we're just cool."

"Uh-huh," Brittany and Shaniqua said, giving each other knowing glances.

They all giggled.

"So what's up guys, what are we going to do next?" Natasha said.

"Well, I think Nate's cute?" Shaniqua said.

"Nate who?" Natasha and Brittany harmonized.

Shaniqua beamed at Natasha. "Your brother."

"Oh, no you don't, Ms. Thang," Brittany said. "You are not about to mess with our transportation!"

"I know that's right!" Natasha said, slapping high-fives with Brittany.

Shaniqua laughed and high-fived both of her best friends.

The End

Did You Know . . .

An average of 28% of high school and college students experience dating violence at some point.

Twenty-six percent of pregnant teens reported being physically abused by their boyfriends. About half of them said the battering began or intensified after he learned of her pregnancy.

The daughters of teen parents are 22% more likely to become teen mothers themselves.

Every year 3 million teens − 1 in 4 sexually experienced teens − acquire an STI (Sexually Transmitted Infection). Yet, less than one-third of sexually active teens have been tested for HIV.

Eighty-seven percent of high school seniors have used alcohol; in comparison, 63% have smoked cigarettes; 32% have used marijuana, and only 6% have used cocaine.

Over 2,000 kids between 16 and 20 years of age die every year in alcohol-related car crashes.

Students with grade point averages of D or F drink 3 times as much as those who earn A's.

The common dominator in all of the negative behaviors listed is lack of self-esteem. As defined by the National Association for Self-Esteem, it is the experience of being capable of meeting life's challenges and being worthy of happiness. People who have healthy or authentic self-esteem trust their own being to be life-affirming, constructive, responsible, and trustworthy.

Sources:

http://www.ptialaska.net/

http://www.mudpc.org/stats.html

http://www.house.gov/roybalallard/ht_underage.html

http://www.campaignforrealbeauty.com/supports.asp?section=&id=93

South Carolina Campaign to Prevent Teen Pregnancy 2005 Fact Sheet: Adolescent Pregnancy Update

South Carolina Campaign to Prevent Teen Pregnancy 2005 UPDATE: HIV/AIDS and Sexually Transmitted Infections

Believe in You!

Ms. Thang Discussion Guide

1. Who was your favorite character(s) and why?

2. Which character can you best identify with and why?

3. What was the most memorable event in the story and why?

4. What are your thoughts about Shaniqua dating Jordan?

5. Explain the potential hazards of Shaniqua skipping school with Jordan.

6. What type of relationship did Natasha and Stephen have? Explain.

7. How do you feel about Brittany's decision to get a ride home from Jared? What would you do in that situation?

8. Do you feel Brittany's parents placed a lot of pressure on her? If so, how?

9. How do you feel the role model and/or negative influences in each girl's lives affected their decisions?

10. How did family values guide the character's decision making process and ultimately affect their families? Explain.

Other books by Sonia Hayes from the ATL Girlz series:

Book I
Ms. Thang
ISBN 978-0-9777573-0-5

Book II
Urban Goddess
ISBN 978-0-9777573-1-2

Book III
Eye Candy
ISBN 978-0-9777573-2-9

T-Shirt Giveaway

One lucky reader will be selected every month to receive a free T-shirt.

❏ Ms. Thang fitted T-shirt
    Size: ❏ S   ❏ M   ❏ L   ❏ XL

❏ Urban Goddess fitted T-shirt
    Size: ❏ S   ❏ M   ❏ L   ❏ XL

Please submit this page to enter. Duplicate entries or photocopies will not be accepted. Please print legibly. You will be notified via e-mail.

Name:_____

Address:_____

City _____State_____Zip_____-___

Email:_____

Please Mail to:
NUA Multimedia
4611 Hardscrabble Road
Suite 109, PMB 309
Columbia, SC 29229

GOOD LUCK!

Q U I C K   O R D E R   F O R M

Fax order: 803.419.8787. *(Send this form.)*
Telephone order: 803.246.5547.
E-mail order: orders@soniahayes.com
Postal order: NUA Multimedia
                      4611 Hardscrabble Road, Suite 109
                      PMB 309
                      Columbia, SC 29229. USA

Have your credit card ready.

Please send the following:

❏ Ms. Thang Novel ($9.95 ea.)

❏ Urban Goddess Novel ($9.95 ea.)

❏ Ms. Thang fitted T-shirt – Size S, M, L, XL ($14.95 ea.)

❏ Urban Goddess fitted T-shirt – Size S, M, L, XL ($14.95 ea.)

Special Offer ~ Buy one book and one shirt for $20.00

Please mail to:

Name:_____

Address:_____

City _____State_____Zip_____-_____

Telephone: _____

Email: _____

Shipping by air:

❏ US: $4 for the first product and $2 for each additional product.

❏ International: $9 for the first product and $5 for each additional
   product. (estimate)

Payment: ❏ Money Order   ❏ Check   ❏ Credit card:
            ❏ Visa   ❏ MasterCard   ❏ AMEX   ❏ Discover

Card number _____

Name on card _____Exp. Date_____

Signature _____